THE CARNIVAL

Also by
Thomas Clark

Noah
The Storm
The Altar Boy

A novel by

THOMAS CLARK

LUMINARE PRESS
WWW.LUMINAREPRESS.COM

The Carnival
Copyright © 2024 by Thomas Clark

All rights reserved. This book or any portion thereof may not be reproduced or used in any manner whatsoever without the express written permission of the publisher, except for the use of brief quotations in a book review.

Printed in the United States of America

Cover Design: CLARKCOMMS.COM

Luminare Press
442 Charnelton St.
Eugene, OR 97401
www.luminarepress.com

LCCN: 2024908894
ISBN: 979-8-88679-561-5

To all the very nice people named Olga.
(I had to name her something.)

1

Before the phone rang, Olga had assumed that Lester was dead, shot by an angry husband or beaten to death by the father of one of the young women in what he referred to as his butterfly collection. He rarely brought the butterflies to watch the women wrestlers he managed in those long-ago days, but when he did, it was hard to believe they belonged to the same race of human beings as the brutes who traveled the circuit with Olga.

"This can't be the Lester Turner I used to know."

"The one and only, my dear."

"Say something that only Lester Turner would know, and maybe I'll believe I'm not having a nightmare."

There was a pause on his end of the phone. "Let me see…"

In the background, Olga heard the god-awful classical music Lester always listened to. She was about to tell him the music was all the proof she needed when he started laughing. "How is this? I was in Joliet, Illinois the night you and Wanda the Wildcat got pissed off at a referee and threw him into the first row."

"Third row," Olga corrected. "What a twerp that asshole was."

"Ah, yes, the good old days," Lester began before catching himself. "But let us save the sharing of such fond memories for another time." He cleared his throat. "Olga, my dear, how would you like to make a good deal of money?"

Olga had the weird feeling that Lester somehow knew she had just finished writing checks to cover, among other things, the carnival payroll, two new tires for her aging Ford Bronco, a shipment of stuffed animals for the arcade games, popcorn and cotton candy supplies, and six new strings of bright yellow lights. The exercise had not cleaned her out, but as always, it made her wonder if she was going to spend the rest of her life worrying about money.

"How much?" Olga asked more eagerly than she intended.

"Let us say, two hundred thousand dollars."

Olga was dumbfounded. Her eyes found the still-open checkbook on the costume trunk she used as a desk. A good gross for a rainless week in the middle of the summer was five thousand dollars. She tried to calculate how many weeks of working and worrying and dragging her outfit from one hick town to another it would take to pile up two hundred thousand dollars. The answer she came up with was somewhere between forever and never. She asked Lester if she had heard him right.

"You did, my dear. Two hundred thousand dollars. Cold cash."

If there was anyone in the world who was not born yesterday, it was Olga Muntz. "And just what do I have to do in return?" she asked suspiciously.

Lester Turner was the craziest human being Olga had ever met. In their years together on the wrestling circuit, she had learned to not be surprised by anything he did or anything he said. None of that prepared her for the "little mission" he had decided Olga, the one-time star of his show, was the perfect person to carry out.

"Do what?" she asked.

He told her again, this time describing in detail a special room he had constructed above the six-car garage at his enormous house on Lake Michigan. "Completely soundproof, water bed, Jacuzzi, mirrors everywhere."

"Lester, you are one sick bastard."

"Always have been, my dear. You know that. The problem is that I have become so old and wrinkled that even with all my money, the only amusements I can lure to my bed chamber are wino hags who bore and disgust me."

"And what exactly are you looking for?"

"I need a new butterfly. Something young and beautiful. I don't believe they make virgins anymore but something along that line."

Though she had already guessed the answer, Olga asked how she fit into this insane plan.

"You are my butterfly net, my dear. In the course of parading your amusing carnival from one hamlet to another, you must encounter numerous young women. Simply pick out one for me, take possession of her, and hold her until I can get down there and collect her."

"And you will pay me two hundred thousand dollars?"

"Cash."

"And why two hundred thousand?" she asked.

"That is what I paid for my last Lamborghini, and based on my extensive experience with such things, a bouncy young woman will give me much more joy than any automobile, no matter how expensive." There was a pause and a sigh. "It is true that I won't be able to trade her in when I'm done with her." He laughed quietly.

"Lester, they call that kind of thing kidnapping. People who do it go to prison for a long time."

"Don't get caught, my dear."

Olga was tempted, very tempted, not only by the money but by the chance to live on the edge again, a thrill she had not experienced since she left the ring. She stared at the dog-eared checkbook lying on the costume trunk. "Three hundred thousand," she told Lester.

"Two-fifty. Upon delivery, my dear."

2

Dark clouds had gathered ominously every afternoon since the Muntz Traveling Carnival rolled into Milford, Delaware, the third stop on a summer trek through small towns and rural crossroads where the siren call of arcade games and spinning rides lured the curious and bored like bugs to a porch light. So far, the rain that the uncertain clouds threatened had held off, and the crowds were decent, bringing in money enough to cover expenses and put a few precious dollars in Olga Muntz's pocket. Rain was the bane of Olga's existence, rain and the dead-beat workers the carnival business attracted. They stole, they drank, and no matter how closely she watched them, they pulled stunts that required her to make donations she could not afford to the local Policemen's Welfare Association or whatever label was attached to the upturned palms that made the problems go away. "Comes with the god-damned territory," Olga grumbled as she rolled down the car window and tossed the remains of her morning cigarillo into the hot summer air. It was not like bright young people were spending their college years learning how to run a shooting gallery or operate a Tilt-A-Whirl. In her business, Olga had to take what she got, and the ones who stuck with her did so with a clear understanding that she was not going to take an ounce of crap from any of them.

Welcome to Maryland, The Old Line State, the sign said. Olga had no idea what that meant, and she wasn't about to look it up. She glanced at the clock on the dashboard of the old Bronco, trying to remember the last time she had rolled out of bed at such an ungodly hour. An amazing orange sun rising over the knee-high fields of corn lining Route 301 went completely unnoticed as Olga eased into a daydream about the fantastic things she was going to do with the pile of money Lester Turner had offered her last night. The insanity of what he wanted her to do did not curb a list of possibilities that got no further than dumping the Bronco and buying a Cadillac Eldorado before her mind wandered back to the reality of what she was doing on the road so early in the morning. To Olga's way of thinking, having to meet with a bunch of hick politicians before they would issue a carnival permit was ridiculous. In all her years in business, that was a first. *And a last,* she told herself. If Lester's crazy plan worked out, early mornings would find her chilling out in a bed fit for a queen.

The Carnival

An overhead sign reminded her to *Drive Gently*. Stupid sayings like that drove Olga crazy. What the hell was *Drive Gently* supposed to mean? Had the idiot who dreamed up that one ever tried to drive a beat-up Ford Bronco *gently*? She was about to stomp on the accelerator and show the great state of Maryland what she thought about their idiotic signs when she spotted the nose of a police cruiser idling in a clump of pine trees. "Nice hiding job, asshole," she muttered, raising her middle finger without letting go of the steering wheel. It was going to be a long day, but if she wanted to keep the next date on her schedule, she had no choice but to sit through the stupid meeting, then get her butt back to Delaware in time to keep the gang of misfits who worked for her from screwing up any worse than they usually did.

As she neared the top of the Chesapeake Bay Bridge, a gust of wind broadsided the Bronco and pushed it far enough into the middle lane to incite a squeal of protest from an unnerved Volkswagen. "Your horn works—try the damned windshield wipers!" Screaming like that, even when no one heard her, was usually relaxing. Olga tried again but it still didn't work.

Through the massive network of bridge trusses, Olga saw gangs of gray clouds menacing the morning sky. Even the threat of rain would mean fewer people at the carnival tonight, and fewer people meant going into the red for the week. Her late father, who loved dispensing words of wisdom with the Iron

City boilermakers he served at his ten-stool bar back in Allentown, had warned her. She hated to admit it, but time had proven that, of all the stupid theories he swore by, one actually made sense: Never invest a nickel in a business that depended on the weather. Owning a golf course, running a hamburger stand at the beach, driving a Good Humor truck, or even owning the Philadelphia Phillies, were examples he'd ticked off to make his point. No doubt he would have added the carnival business to this blacklist if he had still been around when his only child retired from professional wrestling and took up a way of life that came as close as anything she could think of to running away and joining the circus. Her dreams of doing something magical like that had provided windows of escape from her lousy childhood but failed miserably in the details department. It had never rained in those dreams, not once, and there had never been the first hint of bills that had to be paid whether it rained or shined.

Born with the arms and shoulders of a weightlifter and an inhuman degree of determination that her father, in his alcoholic wisdom, declared was the result of her German heritage, Olga had stood toe to toe with every adversary life had thrown at her. This latest challenge, running a traveling carnival, was no tougher than any of the opponents she had encountered growing up or stared down across the wrestling ring. The highlight of her short stay in high school had been knocking four teeth out of the lipsticked mouth of a preppy girl on the cheerleading squad who declared in front of her snickering friends that Olga looked like Quasimodo. Olga had no idea who Quasimodo was, but she knew by the circle of laughter surrounding her that she was being mocked. Four front teeth had been the price that Barbie Doll cheerleader had paid for her wisecrack, only two of which the janitor found on the cafeteria floor. The price Olga paid had been expulsion from high school and eleven months in the Lehigh Valley Juvenile Detention Center.

Those early years instilled in Olga beliefs as unshakable as any religion, and those beliefs embraced only two commandments: Do whatever it takes to get on top and then do whatever it takes to stay there. To her, the magic words were *whatever it takes*, and they were the creed Olga lived by whenever she came face to face with anybody or anything standing in her way.

A green cluster of overhead signs drew close enough to be read. *Route 97*. Her exit. She wedged the Bronco into the right lane, infuriating a semi with an ocean liner horn. "Kiss my ass," she snarled into a rear-view mirror filled with the reflection of a behemoth so close on her tail that she could count the bug splats decorating its huge silver teeth. Olga stomped on the gas pedal, watched the big truck shrink to the size of a toy in her mirror, and settled back into thoughts about the phone call that was her ticket to a way of living that was going to land her butt in a plush Cadillac Eldorado—a metallic silver one, she had decided before falling asleep last night. She was going to find out what pleated leather seats felt like and groove on that wonderful new car smell every time she slipped behind the wheel. And, she reminded the face in the mirror, she was going to have enough money to pay bills without scraping the bottom of her checking account. In the middle of this celebration, it occurred to her for the first time that she might just get the hell out of the carnival business. Olga leaned on the Bronco's horn and pounded the steering wheel. All she had to do was catch Lester Turner a pretty little butterfly.

Last night, without the first concern about the enormity of Lester's proposition, she had begun putting together a plan that even in the light of day seemed like a winner. Step one was to keep an eye out for the type of pretty woman that Lester had never been able to keep his hands off. If one didn't appear while the carnival was still in Delaware, she would look all the harder after setting up shop in Maryland. Step two was cornering the unlucky girl in a very lonely spot and taking her down. The cornering part might be a little tricky, but the takedown would be a snap. Olga had spent her wrestling career immobilizing women as strong as buffalos, and this one, when she found her, would be as helpless as those long-ago high school cheerleaders. She smiled as she thought about reviving her most famous move, the Muntz Strangle Hold. With just the right amount of pressure, it could put a gorilla to sleep. Five seconds was her record: June the Giant, Joplin, Missouri, 1981.

There was still the matter of finding a safe place to keep the precious thing until Lester got his ass down here from Michigan—with the cash, of course—and hauled her away. There was no way Olga could stuff her into the storage closet of her carnival trailer, not with the way the deadbeats on her payroll were constantly popping their heads in the door and asking the kinds of questions only imbeciles could dream up. She had just begun to give that part of the plan serious thought when she spotted a *Route 32 West* sign. She reached for the scribbled note on the passenger seat. That was the road she wanted. The ramp curled under two overpasses and merged onto a westbound highway. Maybe the thing to do was find some out-of-the-way place to rent; maybe even one of those public storage units. It would only be for a few days. A week at the most. The whys and why-nots of that idea were bouncing around in her mind when she saw signs for the Hargrove County offices. The clock on the Bronco's dusty dashboard told her she had time for the jolt of black coffee she needed to survive a meeting with a bunch of simple-minded bureaucrats.

3

Compared to the white-columned courthouse and the limestone-trimmed county office building that shared the same hedge-lined parking lot, the Hargrove County police station was an architectural embarrassment. It had been constructed in the late 1930s to house the few administrative offices required by what was then an agricultural county and to replace a small lending library that had burned to the ground three years earlier. Howard Livingston Crookshaw, proclaimed by the building's weathered cornerstone to have been the building's architect, had either accepted a very low fee to produce the project drawings or had not been given adequate time to utilize whatever design skills he possessed. The blessing of Mr. Crookshaw's career may well have been the fact that he managed to get himself killed by his bookkeeper's husband twenty years before the author of a publication entitled *The Architecture of Hargrove County* labeled his tired pile of bricks "Neo-Mediocre."

The only thing new about the building was the bright, aluminum radio antenna bolted to the roof parapet, an upgrade a tight-fisted county council had no choice but to fund when the old antenna was destroyed by a hurricane a year earlier. That same storm had saturated half the building's ceiling tiles and blown out most of the windows on the wall facing the courthouse. Those windows—five to be exact—remained covered with plywood, a measure described as temporary by the council members while they debated the details of the latest window replacement bids.

The insides of the plywood panels had been imaginatively transformed into a five-panel mural depicting with amazing accuracy the street scene that had previously been visible through the windows. No detail had been omitted, but several had been improved upon. The courthouse lawn was as green and well-tended as a country club fairway, the drab boxwoods lining the base of the county's most-stately building had been replaced by pink and white azaleas in full bloom, and the parking meters lining the sidewalk just outside the windows had magically disappeared. The mural had been completed in her spare time by Helen Burgess, whose official title was police department secretary, a job description that to her way of thinking, did not come close to conveying her importance to T.J. Barnes, the county police chief and his overworked team of deputies. Helen was also an accomplished cultivator of a species of zucchini squash that overran her small backyard every summer, a trivial annoyance considering that the pick of her crop had won two blue ribbons in the last three years at the Hargrove County Fair. Once, in a strange and terrifying dream, Helen had been forced to decide between tending to her zucchinis or working on her paintings. In that dream, after being tied to a post and having a lizard waved in her face, she had agreed to give up the zucchinis, mainly because she was the sitting president of the Hargrove County Art League, a post that satisfied her addiction to being in charge.

"Good, morning, T.J.," Helen sang out at the sight of her boss. "All the telephone messages are on your desk, including one from 'You-Know-Who.'"

Helen had been staring at the mural when T.J. Barnes arrived, wondering what she was going to do with the five big panels when and if the county council came up with the money to replace the windows. The plywood belonged to the county, but the artwork was hers. She decided to ask the county attorney about the legalities of the matter the next time he had business at the police station. The young man's hair was too long to suit Helen's tastes, and he had an annoying habit of constantly checking the time to make sure everyone knew he was the owner of a gold Rolex; other than that, he seemed more normal than a lot of people who worked at the courthouse.

T.J. ignored the "You-Know-Who" comment and slipped into his office.

"Also, that obnoxious Mrs. Eaglebutt called from the county executive's office," Helen called after him. "She ordered me to remind you about the carnival meeting. Eleven o'clock. It's on your calendar."

"Eagleton," T.J. murmured as he shuffled through the messages stacked on his battered desk. "The woman's name is Eagleton."

"Yeah, yeah," Helen replied from the cramped alcove that passed as a reception area. She had ears like a rabbit.

T.J. arranged the messages into three piles. The ones on the left, he would return himself. The ones in the middle, he would tell Helen to give to Nick Suit, who he had recently promoted to corporal. The ones on the right, he would use for trash can target practice.

"Helen," he called through the open door.

She appeared with an outstretched hand. "Nick's on his way in. I'll give them to him when he gets here."

Making no attempt to be sneaky about it, Helen leaned over his desk to see which messages T.J. had saved for himself. There were only two. One was from Jerry Donnelly, the county fire chief, and the other was from Mary Beth Banakowski, the head nurse at St. Joseph's hospital or, in Helenspeak, "Miss You-Know-Who." She flicked her eyebrows knowingly at T.J.

"Probably hospital business," he informed her.

"I've got your hospital business," Helen informed him back. She saluted and left. There was no reason for her to salute. T.J. wished she would knock it off, but Helen got a big kick out of saluting, and T.J. had better things to do than make an issue of it.

"Need to talk before this morning's meeting. Important." was the message that Jerry Donnelly had dictated to Helen. "Important" was underlined twice.

T.J. flipped a coin mentally. Heads, he would call Mary Beth first. Tails, he would call Jerry Donnelly second. He settled back in his chair and dialed the number he knew by heart. "Have you decided?" Mary Beth asked without saying hello.

"Decided what?" T.J. answered, uneasy in his growing conviction that she could read his mind the way she had in another lifetime when she was his whole world.

"Okay." She drew out the word. "Just thought I'd check. My answer is yes. All you have to do is work up the nerve to ask the question."

Jerry Donnelly, the county fire chief, appeared in the doorway. "I've got to run," T.J. said into the phone, motioning for Jerry to take a chair.

"Okay," Mary Beth repeated, this time in a tone that informed T.J. that he wasn't fooling anyone.

"I decided it would be better to talk to you in person," an obviously worried Jerry Donnelly said, removing his chief's hat and searching for a place to park it on T.J.'s overtaxed desk.

T.J. knew exactly what his long-time friend wanted to talk about. He glanced at the clock that hung above a large street map of the jurisdiction they both knew as well as they knew their own backyards. In an hour, the two of them would appear before the county council to answer questions about issuing the Hargrove County Volunteer Fire Department a permit to open its annual carnival next Monday night, an issue the six council members had delayed dealing with as long as they possibly could.

Jerry cleared his throat. "Have you decided what you are going to tell them, T.J.?"

"I'm not sure what I'm going to tell *them*, but what I'm going to tell *you* again, Jerry, is that I'm not ready to have a repeat of what happened the summer before last."

"Christ, T.J., neither am I, and I have given you my word that it won't."

T.J. stood up and walked over to the window behind his desk, one of the few that had survived the hurricane. "Convince me, Jerry."

The veteran fire chief's voice rose in frustration. "We went over all of this last week. I called six fire departments, a Kiwanis Club, and one Knights of Columbus Council that have hired this carnival company, and not one of them had a major complaint. No one said they would invite them into their living rooms, but what the hell, they're carnival people."

There had been no fireman's carnival in the two years since T.J.'s team discovered what the dirtballs

Jerry and his people had hired were doing to maximize their profits. That two-year time-out, the fire department's executive board desperately hoped, would be long enough for the county churches, the PTA, and the local newspapers to forget about what Jerry Donnelly preferred to label "an unfortunate event."

To T.J., what happened two summers ago was a hell of a lot more serious than that. He turned from the window, shaking his head at the thought that there were people who had the balls to think they could pull off a stunt like that right under his nose. Jerry started to say something, but T.J. interrupted. "Give me a second while I make sure I remember everything correctly."

What he was remembering, and what he knew was correct, was that on the second night of that sorry-assed carnival, there had been a fistfight involving an off-duty fireman and a carnival worker who tried to pick his pocket. That was strike one. On the very next night, T.J. received eleven complaints—eleven—about customers being shortchanged by three different carnival employees: a man in a clown suit who sold balloons, the woman who ran the popcorn stand, and her twin sister who sold tickets for the miniature train ride. One or two complaints like that might be written off as he-said-she-said, but eleven in one night? In T.J.'s book, that was at least strike two. In an attempt to prevent any more trouble, he assigned two of his deputies, Mark Jenkins and Sarah Roberts, to mix with the crowd in their street clothes and keep an eye on things.

Strike three generated the kind of headlines Hargrove County did not need. The owner of the carnival company, a man named Lucky Geesler, approached Mark while Sarah was busy watching the Wheel of Fortune operator. He asked if Mark was interested in seeing "the real show."

"The real show," as it turned out, was taking place in a tent pitched behind the carnival's parked trucks. Mark Jenkins had spent four years as an MP in the Marines pulling men out of dives in the four corners of the globe, but the show that took place under a blue spotlight in the center of that tent was one he had difficulty accurately describing to T.J., not to mention testifying about in a crowded courtroom, a performance his fellow police officers refused to let him forget.

Jerry Donnelly lost patience and interrupted T.J. before he had the pleasure of reliving every warm detail of shutting down that carnival and running its sleazy aggregation of fortunetellers and balloon hawkers out of the county.

"T.J., listen to me. Do you know how much money we lost by not holding a carnival the last two summers? It's the fire department's most important fundraising event by far. Our fall auction helps, but that money is nothing compared to what we make from the carnival." Jerry had risen to his feet and was searching for a spot where he could pound his fist on T.J.'s desk. "The woman who owns this new company, Olga Muntz, seems like a tough cookie, I'll grant you that, but we negotiated a damn good deal with her. Listen to this: We get every dollar people spend on the moonwalk, the pony rides, and at the funnel cake tent, and we split the take from the bingo tent fifty-fifty with her. That's a hell of a better deal than we had with that last clown."

He sat back down and took a deep breath. "Help me with the county council this morning, T.J., and I'll owe you big time."

Lieutenant Jenkins rapped on the doorjamb and was halfway into the room before realizing T.J. had someone with him.

"Sorry, Chief. I'll come back."

"It's okay, Mark. What is it?"

The young police officer glanced uncertainly at the county fire chief before answering. "I checked out the last carnival on the list you gave me, the one the Muntz Company ran last August up in Bedford, Pennsylvania."

"And?"

"Turns out it was the Bedford County Sheriff's Department that hired Muntz. It was their annual carnival."

"Interesting. What did the sheriff's department have to say about them?"

"The sheriff himself was on vacation, but I spoke with a Lieutenant..." Mark Jenkins flipped through a manila folder, searching for the man's name. "...a Lieutenant Barber. I asked him if there had been any trouble at the carnival. He told me rather pointedly that nothing happened that they couldn't handle. When I pressed him for details, he got bent out of shape and wanted to know if I thought their department would do business with anyone who didn't respect the law." Mark closed the folder. "I'm afraid that's all I could get out of the guy."

"What's this all about?" Jerry Donnelly asked uneasily.

"The county council ordered me to do a background check on the people you hired to run your carnival this year."

"Okay, sounds like you did that. What's your call?"

"In a perfect world, Jerry, my department would never have to deal with another traveling carnival."

Jerry stood up and smiled at the one person in Hargrove County who had as much responsibility as he did. "In a perfect world, T.J., the fire department would get all the funding it needed from the county council and not have to put on a damn carnival every summer." He turned when he got to the door. "I'm counting on your support this morning."

4

Olga Muntz gave the Bronco an extra shot of gas and blew through a traffic signal that was green enough for her. Two blocks down the road, the Golden Arches of a McDonald's wasted time trying to tempt her. She needed hot coffee in a real cup and an egg sandwich fried on a diner grill.

Large, white arrows suspended above the next intersection pointed left for Saint Joseph's Memorial Hospital and straight ahead for the county offices. "What I need is a goddamned sign that tells me where to find a half-decent breakfast." Olga had barely mouthed the words when she spotted exactly what she was looking for: the Old Line Diner, stainless steel exterior, curved roof, bright orange neon sign. "If a place like this doesn't have what I'm looking for," Olga grumbled, pulling into the parking lot, "then this old girl was never known as The Allentown Amazon."

Inside, the diner reminded Olga of the twenty-four-hour eateries dotting the roads in Western Pennsylvania where her carnival spent the last weeks of its summer run. She dropped into a booth near the door and slipped a plastic-covered menu from its hiding place behind the napkin dispenser, a move the regulars never made. Anything a body needed for breakfast, lunch, or dinner was listed on an illuminated menu board spanning the length of the counter. *Fried egg sandwich with a side of home fries.* There it was. Olga slapped the menu closed and almost managed to look happy when she spotted green-ringed coffee mugs on every table, the final sign that she had come to the right place.

A waitress who looked like she might hold her own in a wrestling ring wiped her hands on a dishtowel and made her way across the room with a friendly smile. "What can I get you?" she asked.

"Cup of coffee, black, and the fried egg sandwich," Olga answered, pointing up at the menu board. "And," she added, "some directions."

"Where to?"

"The county office building."

"Turn right out of the parking lot, then left on Jefferson Street until you hit Courthouse Square. You can't miss it."

"You allow smoking in here?" Olga asked, fingering the box of cigarillos in her jacket pocket.

The waitress shook her head. "County ordinance."

Olga's natural instinct was to argue, but in this case, she didn't. She had already smoked two cigarillos this morning, and while she had never kidded herself about her appearance, the brown teeth look was something she could live without. She watched the broad-shouldered woman squeeze through the packed tables on her way back to the counter. *Wrestling was only part of it,* she thought. *It took more than a strong back and thick arms.* Overnight drives from one stinking arena to another were a drag, dressing rooms the size of closets made it almost impossible to bend over and tie your shoes, and promoters who lied through their teeth about the night's take made for memorable fights the fans never saw. Worst of all, she decided long ago, were the male wrestlers they were forced to travel with, half-human whales who thought of woman wrestlers as playthings with muscles. Olga smiled at the memory of a guy named Carlton the Caveman who missed three shows in Pittsburgh with a bad case of crushed nuts after he made that mistake with her. She was still smiling when her smoking-hot coffee arrived.

"By the way, I'm Sissy," the waitress informed her. "For better or worse, I own this place."

Olga nodded. "Lucky you. I'm in the carnival business. Try that sometime."

"The carnival that's supposed to open here Monday night?"

Olga sipped the coffee, then sipped again. "The carnival that *better* open here Monday night. I have a signed contract and a fat deposit from the fire department."

"Order up. Fried egg sandwich and home fries," the cook hollered from a window behind the counter. "Get it while it's hot."

"There was a lot of trouble at the last fire department carnival," Sissy said, placing Olga's breakfast on the table and sliding the salt and pepper shakers away from the wall. "I saw in the paper last night that the county council still hasn't issued a permit for this one."

"That last carnival wasn't mine, Honey."

"Sissy. It's Sissy."

"What? Oh, yeah, right. By the way, what do you know about the bunch of morons I'm supposed to meet with this morning?"

Sissy didn't know who Olga was talking about and was about to say so when she was distracted by the hurried arrival of a beautiful young woman. "Good morning, Patricia," she called out with a big smile. "Don't tell me, a coffee to go, two creams and two sugars. I'll meet you at the counter." She was grinning with happiness when she turned her attention back to Olga. "Which bunch of morons are you talking about? We have our share around here."

Olga was no longer listening. Her full attention was focused on the young woman whose beauty had just lit up the crowded diner. *Perfect,* she thought. *Absolutely perfect!*

While Olga watched her the way a fox watches a rabbit, the young woman took a seat at the counter and turned to wait for Sissy to join her. *If only Lester Turner was here to see this one,* Olga thought as she downed the last of her coffee. She stood up and walked toward the counter. Her mind was racing. On any other day, it would be a simple matter of following the girl, finding out where she lived or worked, and then coming up with a plan. The problem was that Olga had to get to that damned meeting. She could come back after the meeting and ask about the girl, but that might be something a person like this Sissy would remember later. Olga smiled at the young woman, and the young woman smiled back. Chestnut hair. Perfect teeth. A few freckles on her nose, but Lester would probably get a kick out of a kinky touch of innocence.

Sissy came back with the girl's coffee. "Anything else this morning, Patricia?" she asked.

The girl shook her head. She was wearing a nametag, a hospital nametag. *Patricia Dugan, RN, Saint Joseph's Memorial Hospital.* Olga remembered seeing a sign for the hospital on the way in. A plan seemed to be making itself.

"Here comes your partner, right on time," Sissy announced.

Another young woman, every bit as beautiful as the first one but in a different, dark-hair way, joined Sissy and the girl with the *Patricia* nametag at the counter. "The usual, Sissy, and a dozen bagels to go. It's Friday, my turn to treat the general surgical staff."

"You've got it, Rita. Mix them up?"

"Please, Sissy, except no onion bagels. Dr. Fuller hates onions."

"Well, phooey on Dr. Fuller," Sissy said, reaching for Olga's empty cup. "By the way, Rita, your father came in for lunch yesterday. He was with one of your brothers, but I don't know which one. I can't tell them apart."

"Probably Anthony. He works for my father. Dario is an EMT with the fire department when he's not selling cars for my uncle."

"Well, if that was Anthony, he looks like an Italian movie star."

"Oh, God, don't tell him that! He's tough enough to live with as it is."

Sissy laughed. She had seen Rita Anselmo with her brothers many times, and it was obvious that they were inseparable. She slid Olga's refilled cup across the counter.

"Gotta run," Rita said. "The hospital calls. Coming, Patricia?"

Olga watched the two girls leave. The nurse named Patricia, ivory-skinned and blue-eyed, had caught her eye first, but either of them would be the perfect center of attraction for the weird playroom Lester had constructed above his garage. Olga Muntz was as close to being in a good mood as she ever got. A golden opportunity had fallen right into her lap. All she had to do was play her cards right, and Lester

Turner would have his new butterfly, and one old wrestler would be swimming in a pile of money. Not even meeting with a bunch of small-town numbnuts could ruin this day.

5

Olga climbed back into the Bronco feeling like she had hit the jackpot. "Come on, come on," she ordered an unbroken line of traffic as she waited to pull out of the diner parking lot. "I have a meeting to get to and a trap to set for a very pretty nurse."

Still it came, a parade of cars followed by a herd of trucks. She cursed them all until she became distracted by the thought of how perfect the young nurse was; so perfect, in fact, that she began thinking interesting thoughts about the price tag. Three hundred thousand struck her as a much better number than 250 thousand. Lester could afford it; she knew he could. Back when his hobbies included managing a string of women wrestlers, people were always saying that Lester Turner had more money than God. Olga had never wasted a lot of time wondering whether there was a God, much less how much money He had, but she did know that Lester's father, or maybe it was his grandfather, had made an absolute fortune manufacturing some damned thing.

She spotted a gap in the traffic and was about to stomp on the gas when a sign directly across the road caught her eye. Under a big white *H* were the words *Saint Joseph's Memorial Hospital* with an arrow pointing in the opposite direction from the county office building. Her strong hands tightened on the steering wheel as she remembered that was the name of the hospital on the nurses' nametags. She checked the time. If she didn't go straight to the meeting, she was going to be late. A very short debate ended with the conclusion that the only thing she would miss by being late was a bunch of small-town politicians wiping their glasses and clearing their throats. She spun the steering wheel to the left and bulled her way through screeching brakes and blaring horns. There was a money-making plan to work out, and this was as good a time to start as any.

Seconds after flashing yellow lights warned Olga that she was entering a hospital zone, the screaming siren and whirling rays of an ambulance blew past her and swerved into a driveway marked *Emergency Room*. Olga kept driving, remembering that the nurse with the dark hair had said something about the general surgical unit. She slowed at a *Main Entrance* sign and pulled into an enormous parking lot peppered with tall trees and taller pole lights. The forest of lights told her that the takedown would have to happen somewhere away from the hospital. That was note number one. She eased the Bronco into a space several rows from the hospital's glass-door entrance, getting a kick out of the fact that she had chosen the word *takedown* for what she was going to do. The expression reminded her of the years she had spent battling the likes of Georgia the Gorilla and her famous fingernails and The Texas Time Bomb, a six-foot-five ape with body odor so bad that Olga couldn't stand being on the same bus with her, much less tangling with her in the ring. The prey she was after now would be a piece of cake compared to handling beasts like those two. The takedown itself would not be the challenge. Doing it quickly and quietly so that the precious little thing disappeared without a trace was going to be the name of the game.

Olga lit a cigarillo, opened a notebook that existed only in her head, recorded a reminder about the parking lot lights, and began a list of questions. Did the nurses come and go through those glass doors? Seeing a gang of them hurry into what appeared to be the main lobby told her that the answer to that question was yes. What time did their shift end? Olga smoked and thought. She looked at the dashboard clock. Based on the time the two nurses had hurried out of the diner, it was a pretty good guess that their shift started at nine. She did a little more smoking and a little more thinking. During her days in the ring, she had spent a fair amount of time in hospitals, getting sewed up and having plaster casts slapped on her arms and legs. She smiled, sidetracked by the thought of how the crowds loved the way she learned to use those casts as weapons in the ring. *Twelve hours,* she remembered, getting back to her notes. Nurses in hospitals worked twelve-hour shifts. Two or three of them had told her that. They didn't especially like the long hours, but they loved having four days off every week. An idiot could figure out that if a nurse started at nine in the morning, she would get off at nine at night. The picture was coming together. Her mind drifted, picturing the takedown: the frightened eyes, the disbelief, the futile seconds of kicking and screaming until, with her vise-like arms, she applied the Muntz Strangle Hold. *Just enough pressure—not too much*—she reminded herself, and the pretty little nurse would go out like a light.

She scanned the hospital grounds. Yellow ribbon and orange cones outlined a construction area in front of the main entrance that was alive with workers in hard hats, two dump trucks, and a grunting piece of digging equipment. Olga blew a spiral of smoke through the car window, taking it all in. She would come back for another look or two after she brought the carnival down from Delaware, but she was sure the construction would not be a problem. The workers would be done for the day and drinking beer at a bar somewhere long before her target came strolling through those glass doors. She slipped the Bronco into gear. There was a lot more to think about, but she was already late for a meeting. Not that she gave a particular shit.

The Carnival

On her way back, Olga passed the diner again. *Left on Jefferson Street,* she reminded herself, checking street signs. After the meeting was over, she would look around for a place to stash the goods until Lester showed up with the money. *Something close to the carnival but not too close,* she told herself. *Rent it by phone and pay with cash,* she continued, impressed that she was taking to this new game as naturally as she had taken to the ring.

6

Most of the citizens of Harford County, Maryland were too busy waging war on crabgrass and organizing soccer carpools to fully comprehend the incompetence of the people they elected to public office.

A vocal minority of the county's population, activists with time on their hands and malcontents with chronic cases of bug-up-the-ass, considered the county council and the county executive not only incompetent but borderline criminal, a collection of nitwits whom the founding fathers would have clamped in stocks and pelted with garbage. The most zealous arm of these agitators, The Daughters of Decency, was mobilizing in front of the county office building when Olga pulled into the parking lot. Their bright yellow shirts bore the word *CARNIVAL* with a bold, red line struck through it. The entire group, except for one very large woman with a base drum, was armed with tambourines. Olga leaned on her horn to clear a parking place.

"Are you with us, Sister?" one of the yellow-shirted women made the mistake of asking Olga as she elbowed her way through their buzzing ranks.

"Get your fat ass out of my way," Olga snarled, swatting away a pamphlet that had been stuck in her face.

A security guard stationed at the top of the building's granite steps was the next person to risk a body slam. "Name?" he barked, sliding his paunchy body between Olga and the massive entrance doors.

"Me?"

"Yes, you." He brandished a clipboard to impress her with his authority. "This meeting is closed except to those whose names are on this list." The menace in Olga's narrowed eyes made him nervous enough to add, "By order of the county council."

Olga flexed muscular shoulders twice as wide as his and turned her back on the man. Across the broad expanse of her satin jacket, the words *Muntz Traveling Carnival* were stitched in gold.

The guard ran a shaky finger down the short list of invited participants. "Are you Olga Muntz?" he asked.

"I ain't the Easter Bunny."

The man, a retired bus driver and maternal uncle of the county executive, elected to take that for a yes rather than start an argument with a woman who appeared to be a cross between a weightlifter and a roller derby queen. He stuck the clipboard under his arm and struggled to push open the heavy doors.

Beyond a high-ceilinged lobby, a cavernous meeting room was empty except for the six people seated at a polished wood dais and the two uniformed men who stood before them. Olga stiffened at the sight of the law and slipped into a seat halfway down the side aisle. It wasn't fear; she had never been afraid of anything. It was an animal-like wariness of anyone in the opposite corner of the ring. *Breath slow and easy,* she told herself. *Remember that all any of these clowns know about Olga Muntz is that she runs a carnival business, and that is all they are ever going to know.*

One of the men up front, the one seated behind the biggest brass nameplate, was clearly agitated. "As I reminded everyone when we began," he complained, attempting to sound authoritative, "the sole purpose of this special meeting is to decide whether or not to issue a permit authorizing..." He looked down at his notes and began reading. "...the Muntz Traveling Carnival Company to operate such business on behalf of the Hargrove County Volunteer Fire Department, said carnival to run continuously from Monday, June 13th through Saturday, June 25th on the Hargrove County carnival grounds." He shook a finger at the police officer standing at the microphone. "Chief Barnes, you will confine your remarks to that specific subject and save your usual complaints about the police department budget for the next regularly scheduled meeting of this body. Is that clear?"

T.J. Barnes leaned close to the microphone. "Mr. Babcock, does that include my requesting funds to cover the extra man-hours required to direct traffic and provide security at the carnival you are talking about?"

"That is *County Executive* Babcock to you, Chief Barnes, and yes, you are to refrain from any mention whatsoever of police department funding."

Resisting an ever-present temptation to address the county executive as Skinny, the name the thin balding man had been known by since grade school, T.J. opened a manila folder and, after finding his place, began to read in a clear, deep voice that Skinny Babcock had always envied. "At the council's request, my department conducted a background check on the Muntz Traveling Carnival. In the course of that investigation, we contacted and questioned six organizations and municipalities who have contracted with the subject company in the past two years."

"Finally, we are getting somewhere," the county executive piped. "Please proceed."

T.J. did. "While not uncovering any incidents that in and of themselves would cause my department to recommend against approving this application, our investigation did uncover a number of issues that we feel should be addressed by the company owner before a permit to operate a carnival in Hargrove County is issued." He looked around the room. "It was my understanding that the owner of the carnival company would be here today to answer those questions. Is that you, Madam?" he asked, pointing across the room.

"I am running this meeting, Chief Barnes!" Skinny complained. He pointed at Olga. "Is that you, Madam?"

Olga stood, turned her back on the county council, and let the gold lettering on the back of her purple jacket do the talking. There was something about her cocksure manner that Skinny Babcock found extremely appealing. He was wondering why the name Olga Muntz sounded familiar when he noticed Hastings Dew tapping his watch.

"Ah, yes, Councilman Dew. You have a busy day. I will speed things up by questioning Miss Muntz myself." He motioned for Olga to come to the microphone while he scanned the copy of T.J.'s report that he had been given. "Miss Muntz," he began, glancing over the top of his dark-rimmed glasses, "it says here that in the past three years, six incidents of pickpocketing were reported at your carnival, incidents that were traced to a carnival employee who operated the Ferris wheel."

Olga interrupted him. "I fired that bum the night the cops hauled his ass away and ran the Ferris wheel myself until I found someone else to do it. I can operate every ride I own, and I can repair them if I have to."

What a woman, Skinny Babcock thought. His wife, Babbs, was incapable of changing a light bulb. He scanned the rest of T.J.'s report. Five police responses for fist fights, four arrests for public drunkenness, and two cars vandalized in the carnival parking lot. He raised his eyes again, noticing that Olga's shoulders were as wide as those of the police chief she had muscled away from the microphone. His mind drifted toward some very kinky thoughts before he regained his focus and turned his attention to T.J.

"Chief Barnes," he commented dismissively, "compared to what took place at the last fire department carnival, the list in front of me looks like an investigation of the Hargrove Garden Club."

T.J. started to speak but was interrupted by Councilman Wigglesworth. "I have already made up my mind," he announced into his microphone. Councilman Dew nodded in agreement, checking his watch.

"Councilmen, please," Skinny Babcock protested. "We have not completed the hearing."

"Council*persons*," interjected June Buggs-Vosbeck, the newest member of the council.

"Excuse me?" Skinny asked.

"The term is council*persons*. You officially acknowledged that at our last meeting."

Skinny longed for the days when mailmen were mailmen, handymen were handymen, firemen were firemen, and people were named either Buggs *or* Vosbeck, not Buggs-Vosbeck. He forced a smile at the only council*person* with a hyphenated name and told Olga she could return to her seat. "Speaking of fire*persons*," he continued in an unappreciated attempt at wit, "Fire Chief Donnelly, you have the floor."

Before Jerry Donnelly took the microphone, T.J. attempted to inquire about the status of the police station window replacement and was gaveled to silence. "Fire Chief Donnelly, you have the floor," the county executive repeated with voice-cracking emotion.

The brass buttons on Jerry Donnelly's blue uniform shimmered in the chamber's bright lights as the longtime fire chief of Hargrove County unfolded a list of notes and pressed it flat against the lectern. "First of all," he began, "as I have done many times since the unfortunate events of the summer before last, let me extend a sincere apology to the citizens of our county and repeat once more that the fire department had no idea that any improper activity was taking place on the carnival grounds. I can't stress that point often enough."

"It was absolutely disgraceful," wailed Councilperson Buggs-Vosbeck, shaking her head.

"It was indeed," Councilperson Wigglesworth seconded. "I'm voting *no*."

"You can't vote yet," Skinny declared, rapping his gavel for emphasis. "Fire Chief Donnelly, I assume you were about to explain to this council why you feel we should approve this carnival permit."

"It's very simple," Jerry Donnelly stated. "Without the carnival, the Hargrove County Volunteer Fire Department will require significant additional funding from this council."

The mention of additional funding seemed to startle the council members. "How much?" interrupted Councilperson Warren Smallwood, who had until that moment appeared to be asleep.

The fire chief tapped his notes. "Between not holding the carnival last year and losing the motorcycle raffle that goes with it, we lost approximately forty-five thousand dollars. If you think I'm exaggerating, I can show you the figures."

Forty-five thousand dollars rang a bell with Skinny Babcock. It was the exact amount he was planning to ask the council to approve for the acquisition of a more appropriate mode of official transportation than the small, white Chevy he had been issued.

"One of our pumper trucks is on its last legs," Jerry Donnelly continued. "It is critical that we order a new one, and the only way we can reduce the amount of money this council will have to appropriate for its purchase is to proceed with this year's carnival."

Back in her seat, Olga had stopped listening. She had not gotten up with the birds and driven all the way down from Delaware to listen to a bunch of dimwits argue about fire trucks. She reopened her mental notebook and picked up where she had left off at the hospital. The next order of business, if this meeting ever ended, was to find a safe place to stash Lester's new plaything until he showed up with the money. Her thoughts had just wandered once more to the subject of raising the price tag when she was interrupted.

"Miss Muntz! Miss Muntz!"

Olga had no idea how many times the simpleton who was running the meeting had called her name, but everyone was looking at her. "Would you please step up to the microphone once more?" he continued politely when she looked at him. "The council would like to know if there is anything you would like to add to this proceeding before we vote on the permit application."

The police chief stepped away from the microphone as Olga approached. He looked like he was more of a man than all the wimpy council guys put together, but that didn't bother her. No man she had ever encountered had proved to be much of a threat.

"You have the floor," the man behind the big nameplate informed her. "In your own words, please tell us why the county council should approve this carnival permit."

Her reason for wanting them to approve the carnival permit had changed the moment she saw that beautiful young nurse at the diner. She needed to be here in Maryland, close to the hospital, so she could do what she had to do to get her hands on Lester's money. She had to think of something to say that would hit home with this bunch of dummies. Her mind spun through the possibilities and landed on the word "money." From what she had heard so far, it was obvious that money was all these clowns thought about: money for a new fire truck, money for the big police chief to run his department. As she was about to open her mouth, she remembered the guarantee.

Olga crossed her muscular arms and fixed her eyes on the council members one at a time. "It's pretty simple, the way I see it," she informed them calmly. "I have a contract signed by your fire chief. That man right there." She pointed at Jerry Donnelly as though she were identifying the guilty party at a trial. "And that little old contract states in plain English that this county owes me ten thousand dollars if the carnival is canceled less than sixty days before the scheduled opening date." She looked up into the high ceiling as though she were checking an imaginary calendar. "This is, what, three days before the opening date? If you are not going to approve the permit, just tell me where to pick up the check."

The looks on the faces behind the nameplates told Olga that she had hit the bullseye, but before any of them could speak, the security guard from out front burst into the room and bolted the doors behind him. "They're coming!" he shouted. "Those crazy women with the yellow tee shirts! I tried to stop them, but I couldn't."

The doors began to shake, sending the guard scurrying for cover. From the lobby, a pounding base drum underlined the chant of The Daughters of Decency. "No more carnivals! No more sin! No more carnivals! No more sin!"

"Chief Barnes, do something!" cried the county executive. "This is what we pay you for!"

T.J. Barnes spoke calmly into the microphone. "Stay calm, Skinny. I've got this."

"You want some help?" Olga asked, taking off her satin jacket. "I'd love a crack at that big elephant with the drum."

"You stay here," he told her, heading for the rattling doors.

The council members retreated to the safety of their private chambers where a hurried discussion about the cost of new pumper trucks and ten-thousand-dollar guarantees ended with the unanimous approval of the carnival permit followed by a mass exit across the loading dock at the rear of the building.

"She seems like a decent sort," Skinny Babcock remarked about Olga Muntz as he directed Councilperson Buggs-Vosbeck past the dumpster. It was a statement he would later claim was taken out of context.

7

Mary Beth Banakowski was updating the patient roster on her computer screen when an increasingly regular visitor appeared at her office door, a visitor who had no clue how capable he was of driving her crazy.

"Well, if it isn't the chief of police. Let me guess, you were here at the hospital on official business and just dropped by to say hello."

T.J. Barnes hid his embarrassment with the same boyish smile she remembered so well from high school. "As a matter of fact," he began, retreating into the lines he had rehearsed on the drive over, "I was downstairs in the emergency department interviewing the victim of an assault at a bowling alley." He had no idea where the detail about the bowling alley had come from, but he was pleased with it. What he wasn't pleased with was the uncomfortable fact that the same guy who once had no problem knocking heads with all comers on the football field had once again lost the nerve to ask a woman out to dinner; a woman he had known almost all his life. *Just punt and try it again some other time,* he told himself, walking to the window and adjusting the slant of the blinds. "What's going on down there?" he asked.

"Down where?" Mary Beth answered without looking away from her computer.

"All that excavation work in front of the main entrance."

Mary Beth tapped the save keys on her keyboard and turned to see that T.J. was looking into the hospital's main parking lot.

"Oh, that. A wealthy author named Martha Richardson donated a pile of money to Saint Joseph's with the stipulation that half of it was to be used to construct a small plaza dedicated to the memory of her mother who was a nurse."

"A plaza?"

"With a fountain and some benches. I saw the architect's drawings," she said, checking the chart on her screen. "It's going to be very nice, but it's the last thing the hospital board would choose to spend money on. The upside is that we are free to spend the other half of the money on things we really need."

"Was her mother a nurse here?" T.J. asked, raising the blinds to get a better look.

"No. Apparently, she spent her entire career as a nurse at a hospital in Washington that was torn down years ago. Be careful of those African Violets."

"Looks like they're doing a lot of digging."

"Somebody said they hit an old spring and have to replace a lot of the soil. I just hope they don't make too much noise while they are doing it."

A nurse appeared in the doorway but stopped when she saw T.J.'s police uniform.

"I can come back, Mrs. Banakowski."

"It's okay, Rita, come in."

The young woman smiled uncertainly at T.J. before addressing Mary Beth. "Do you need me to work any extra hours while Patricia is out?"

"God bless you for asking, but I have one of the part-timers filling in for her."

"Okay, I just wanted to check." She glanced again at T.J., apparently wondering what a policeman was doing in her boss's office.

"Before he makes a dumb joke about why he is here, let me introduce you to our esteemed police chief, T.J. Barnes."

Rita's face lit up. "I think my father knows you."

"Really? Who is your father?"

"Vito Anselmo."

T.J. smiled. "Big Vito is your father? Please tell him I said hello."

Rita promised she would, told Mary Beth she was on her way down to the pharmacy, and left.

"Small world," T.J. remarked after she was gone. "I don't actually know her father that well. We played football against each other when he was at Penn State and I was at Maryland."

"It's an even smaller world than that. Vito Anselmo's construction company is building that new plaza downstairs."

"I thought he owned a concrete company."

"Whatever he owns, they won the bid to do the work."

"The rich get richer."

"Tell me about it," Mary Beth said, putting one final touch on the schedule and hitting the keys that saved it. "You should see the house where the Anselmo family lives."

Mary Beth's phone rang before she could explain that the Anselmo family lived right across the street from the home that she and her late husband, Wade Banakowski, had built, a structure, she was embarrassed to realize, every bit as big as the Anselmo house. When she hung up, she changed the subject.

"Mr. Police Chief, you haven't gotten around to telling me what you are doing here. Aside from your bowling alley story, that is." She smiled and waited.

Looking out the window again, T.J. dodged the question. "The author who made that donation must have made a lot of money. What kind of books does she write?"

"Nothing you would have a clue about."

"Try me."

Mary Beth turned slowly in her chair until she was looking directly at T.J. "Martha Richardson writes romance novels," she informed him. "Let me see if I can remember any of the plots." She looked up at the ceiling and struck a thoughtful pose. "Oh, yes; one I especially enjoyed was about this big, strong man who likes a woman very much but can't get up the nerve to ask her out on a date. I can't quite remember how that one turned out."

She knew by the strange way T.J.'s speechless mouth opened and closed that her not-so-subtle dagger had hit home. *If he didn't get the message that time,* she told herself, *he was never going to get it.*

8

Cross the railroad tracks, drive to the top of the hill, then take a right at the florist shop, the directions to the carnival grounds read. Olga checked the Bronco's rearview mirror to make sure the caravan of folded tents and dismantled rides was keeping up with her.

Even though the gate at the railroad crossing was up, and the warning lights were quiet, Olga slowed and looked both ways before leading her parade across the tracks. There were many ways to leave this world, she was fully aware of that, but being run over by a train would be one of the bad ones. She was still trying to imagine what it would be like to be crushed to death by a locomotive when she noticed a sign trying desperately to hold its head above the summer weeds. CHURCH FOR SALE OR LEASE, it read in sun-bleached letters almost obliterated by the word *SINNER!* that was spray-painted over them in angry red strokes. She slowed, causing the vehicles behind her to hit their brakes. *Who the hell sells a church?* she wondered, spotting a weather-beaten steeple and the

THE CARNIVAL

pointed tops of arched windows hiding in the distant trees. The procession had just started up again when the beginnings of an idea began to stir. She wanted to stop and think more about it, but there was a carnival to set up, rides to test, and game tents to stock. At the florist shop, she flipped on the Bronco's turn signal and checked in the mirror one more time to make sure the idiots who worked for her were still there.

By the time the caravan reached Fairgrounds Road, Olga was completely focused on the old church. What better place could there be to stash Lester Turner's new plaything until he showed up with the money that was going to turn the carnival business into a distant memory? Her ideas had bounced from abandoned houses to rental storage units and from barns and garages to RVs and woodsheds, but it never once dawned on her that the last place anyone would look for a missing nurse was in a church.

Olga had no way of knowing that she was not the first sinner to be attracted to the church on Woodyard Road for reasons that had nothing to do with spreading the holy word. The first was Elijah Wise, the founder and pastor of The Church of Christ's Anointed, an evangelical flock of zealots that had been forced to abandon the steepled structure when Elijah surrendered to at least two of the vices he denounced every Sunday morning and took off for parts unknown with Clara Hartman, the church's widowed organ player, and every penny of the 743 dollars in the congregation's bank account. The Reverend Wise's moral lapses may have been grievous enough to incur the wrath of both God and the law but what Olga was about to do would make the missing prelate look like a wayward altar boy.

"We open tomorrow," Olga hollered at her troops after the tents and rides were secured for the night and the last of a hundred awestruck kids chased away. "If you're too hungover to work or end up in a jail cell, you better have the money to buy a bus ticket back to whatever hole you crawled out of because I will forget I ever knew you."

There was a chorus of grumbling and several concealed finger waves, but no one complained loud enough to be heard. Wearing a sleeveless tee shirt that read *Seattle Wrestlemania 1990*, Olga watched them gripe their way to the dormitory busses before she climbed a ladder to adjust one of the dozen speakers whose job it was to blare exaggerations about the quality of the hot dogs and funnel cakes and repeat endlessly that there were bingo prizes that had to be seen to be believed. She slipped the wrench into her back pocket after locking down the final bolt and surveyed what, thanks to Lester and his addiction to pretty girls, would be the next-to-last carnival she would ever have to worry about. Next to last. To avoid raising eyebrows, she would have to haul her pile of headaches to the last stop on the summer schedule, but after that... *After that,* she repeated to herself, flexing rarely used smile muscles, *the rest of my life is going to be lived on Easy Street.*

As she was about to start down the ladder, the late afternoon sun called her attention to a pointed steeple hiding in the trees at the back of the lot. The old church was even closer to the carnival grounds than she thought it was.

"Welcome to Hargove County, Miss Muntz. I'm Jerry Donnelly, fire chief," a man in uniform announced, reaching his hand up to Olga. "We met at the county council meeting."

Olga loved to squeeze men's hands until they flinched.

"Quite a grip you have there," Jerry managed.

With the church begging for a visit, Olga did not have time for small talk. "What can I do for you?" she asked impatiently.

Jerry flashed his big, Irish smile and reminded Olga that her contract with the fire department called for a motorcycle raffle on the last night of the carnival.

"I can read," Olga answered.

The Irish smile faded but only for a second. "A couple of the guys from the station are bringing the bike over here tomorrow so people can get a good look at it. Helps to sell tickets."

"Fine."

The big summer sun was sliding toward a bank of dark clouds on the horizon, subtracting precious minutes from the daylight Olga needed to slip through the woods and see if she could find a legible phone number on the weathered sign she had passed that morning. Making arrangements to use the church without making anyone suspicious was going to be a little tricky, but Olga wasn't worried about it. Something would come to her.

The man with the fire chief hat tucked under his arm had not moved. "If you're done, I've got things to do," Olga informed him as she climbed down from the ladder.

Jerry Donnelly looked over his shoulder to make sure they were alone. "Mrs. Muntz," he started, "I'm sure you heard at the council meeting that there was a lot of trouble at the last carnival."

"So?"

Clearly uncomfortable, Jerry rolled his eyes and made gestures with his hands intended to help Olga get the point. She gave no sign that they did.

"It's just that," he finally managed, "if there is any trouble, this time, the county will never let us have another carnival."

"You have nothing to worry about."

Jerry put on his hat and snapped the brim with his fingers. "Thank you," he said as he turned to leave. "I just wanted to make sure we had an understanding."

Olga watched the man until his bright red car

pulled out of the carnival grounds, then turned to find her way through the woods to the place where the only person with anything to worry about would be caged like a captured bird until a man named Lester Turner showed up with the loot.

9

As opening night approached, objections to the fire department carnival weakened like New Year's resolutions.

"Nobody told me they had a Flying Saucer ride," one middle-aged man bellowed when he came across a half-page carnival advertisement in *The Hargrove Herald*. "I haven't ridden one of those in years."

His wife, who had stayed up late the night before working on a *GO HOME CARNIVAL* banner, looked over his shoulder and saw the words *Funnel Cakes*, a passion she had not indulged since the last carnival. "The least we can do is show our support for the fire department," she mused. "They did keep our house from burning down the day I left the chicken pot pie in the oven."

Posters tacked to telephone poles and taped to store windows, their borders striped in orange and yellow, announced the arrival of *BINGO!*, *ARCADE GAMES!*, and *RIDES, RIDES, RIDES!* "Take us! Take us!" children who were old enough to read begged until their parents relented on the standard conditions that bedrooms be straightened up and lawns cut before they heard one more word about it.

Even the weather, Olga Muntz's tireless foe, had second thoughts. The thunderstorms predicted for opening night never materialized. A beautiful evening unfurled, and so many people headed for the carnival grounds that T.J. Barnes had to assign three officers to handle the traffic. Helen Burgess got stuck in the backup on her way home from the police station and decided to join them rather than fight them. Her decision proved to be the right one when she won a giant stuffed panda by catapulting a rubber frog onto a gold lily pad, a feat she equated to pitching a no-hitter against the New York Yankees.

Despite the waning anti-carnival flack, Jerry Donnelly decided to put a final blessing on the proceedings by asking County Executive Skinny Babcock to preside at a ribbon-cutting ceremony. It was an opportunity that Skinny, a man who relished any opportunity to be the center of attention, jumped at, especially since it would give him a great opportunity to ask Olga Muntz to autograph some pictures of her as The Allentown Amazon that he had found on the internet.

Her name had rung a bell when she appeared at the permit hearing, but it wasn't until later that night while he was googling on his computer that he realized who she was. Skinny had been a huge fan of women's wrestling and lamented its disappearance from the television listings. He loved the big, sweating bodies and the muscular arms and legs of women who seemed to be from a different planet than his wife, Babbs. Olga had been his favorite, the toughest of them all and the star of his most secret fantasies.

"What do you have there?" June Buggs-Vosbeck, who had insisted on being included in the ceremony, demanded like a suspicious schoolteacher as she and Skinny waited for two firemen to stretch a wide blue ribbon across the arched carnival entrance.

"Nothing."

"Don't tell me nothing," she scolded. "Let me have that!"

Of all the pictures of Olga that Skinny had found on his computer, the one that froze June Buggs-Vosbeck was by far his favorite. In it, a snarling Olga, wearing her skin-tight Allentown Amazon costume, had lifted The Panther Woman over her head and was about to throw her out of the ring.

"That is totally disgusting," June Buggs-Vosbeck hissed as the newspaper photographers positioned them for the ribbon cutting.

During the investigation of the savage acts that were about to horrify the community, a cleaning woman reported finding pictures of Olga Muntz under the blotter on Skinny Babcock's desk. Skinny would manage to squirm out of the legal spotlight that followed but paid dearly at home when his wife Babbs canceled their internet service.

In the meantime, the blue ribbon drifted to the sawdust-covered ground, strings of yellow lights lit the evening sky, and the carnival that Hargrove County would never forget opened for business.

The Daughters of Decency, still fuming over the county council's approval of the carnival permit, were the last holdouts. They arrived in a horn-honking caravan and attempted to block the parking lot entrance, an act of civil disobedience that crumbled when T.J. Barnes's people informed them with straight faces that extra copies of their mug shots would be available at a nominal cost.

Rose Duffy, the group's base drummer, demonstrated her commitment to the cause by wrestling the instrument from the roof of a battered Volvo and marching into the opening-night crowd, pounding away with one hand and handing out *Satan Loves Carnivals* pamphlets with the other. To her amazement, no one seemed to care. The polite few who accepted the pamphlets took a quick glance and let them drop to the trampled grass.

"You can either pick up all that damn litter, Drum Girl, or find out what happens if you don't," Olga threatened above the din of loudspeaker music and the exaggerated sales pitches of her game sharks.

Rose was big, but she wasn't tough. She stashed her drum between the shooting gallery and the Whac-A-Mole tent and went to work. Bending over to retrieve the trampled pamphlets hurt her back, but fearing a return of the meanest-looking female she had ever seen, Rose kept at it until she spotted her granddaughter, Olivia, waiting in the miniature car line. Fear of the carnival woman was one thing, but the love of a grandmother for her grandchild was something else entirely. She pushed her way through the crowd and planted a kiss on Olivia's cotton candy-stained face.

"It's no use," Rose complained to her son as they watched Olivia hop into a green roadster and grab a cord attached to the silver bell on its hood. "No one cares about the evils hidden by these bright lights."

"Relax, Ma. Look at that smile on your granddaughter's face."

When the ride was over, Olivia jumped into her grandmother's arms. The taste of cotton candy kisses convinced Rose that her family was the only cause worth getting worked up about. She gave her precious Olivia an extra hug.

"We are going to try to win a goldfish," the young girl cried, wiggling free. "Come with us. Please, please, please!"

The carnival protest was over as far as Rose Duffy was concerned. A workshop dealing with the living conditions of free-range chickens was scheduled for next week. Lukewarm feelings on the subject made Rose feel guilty, but even if she decided to go to bat for the chickens, it would be on one condition: The Daughters of Decency were going to have to find someone else to pound the drum. She was tired of the headaches.

On the way to the goldfish tent, they were stopped by a fireman. "Take a chance on a beautiful Harley Davidson?" he asked, waving a handful of raffle tickets. "Only five dollars for a book of six."

"What exactly is a Harley Davidson?" Rose asked, embarrassing her son.

"It's a motorcycle, Mom. A really cool one."

Rose had even less use for a motorcycle than she had for her drum, but the young man looked so handsome in his uniform, and the ticket money did go to the fire department that only last March rescued her cat Samson from the roof of the Baileys' garage. "I'll take a book," she decided, opening her purse.

10

"Looking for the perfect place to hold your next church revival?" the suit-and-tie guy grinned as he slipped out of a big Lexus and navigated his polished shoes through the parking lot weeds.

Olga thanked him silently for the perfect cover story. "Thinking about it," she replied. "I only need a place for a couple of weeks."

"That would be an unusually short lease period," he began before remembering all the time and effort his company had wasted trying to lease a rundown church that shook to its foundation every time a train rumbled through the crossing at the bottom of the hill. "Let me show you around," he recovered, offering a hand that Olga found disgustingly soft.

"One other thing you should know," Olga said as the heavy front doors creaked open. "My flock does not believe in signing legal documents or writing checks. We pay for everything with cash." At moments of brilliance like this, Olga wondered where she might have ended up if she had not been thrown out of high school.

Dusty shafts of light and the squeal of scurrying rats reminded Olga of the horror movies she loved. "A little elbow grease and this place will be perfect for your revival," the realtor announced, brushing cobwebs from the sleeves of his meticulously pressed jacket.

"Is there a basement?" Olga asked, spotting what appeared to be a door in a dark corner. "We will need storage space for our extra bibles and religious pamphlets."

At the bottom of a steep flight of stairs, an ancient boiler hovered like a rusting beast. A rotting army cot filled the space between one side of the boiler and a damp stone wall. In the corner farthest from the stairs, a dim circle of light from a hanging bulb outlined a freestanding toilet that had been installed long ago for a janitor who was holy enough to mop the church floors but not quite holy enough to use the upstairs bathroom. "Perfect," Olga decided. "Just perfect." All she had to do was replace the broken lock at the top of the stair with a good throw-bolt, and the cellar would be as escape-proof as a dungeon.

"Two weeks," Olga repeated as the two of them climbed back up the stairs. "Two weeks and all cash."

The man excused himself and went out to his car to make a phone call. When he returned, he shook hands with Olga and smiled a happy real estate smile. "Two weeks," he said.

"You've got a deal," Olga answered, tempted to crush his soft hand for the hell of it.

It had been a coin flip, but Olga's mind was made up. The nurse with the powder-white skin and reddish-brown hair would be Lester Turner's new butterfly. Like a cat zeroing in on a mouse, Olga had studied the girl's every move and was ready to take her down. With the old church lined up and a heavy deadbolt now on the cellar door, it was show time. The sooner she made her move, the sooner Lester Turner would appear with the stacks of money that were going to change her life.

On the carnival grounds, business was as good as it had ever been, meaning if Olga didn't keep a sharp eye on things, dollar bills would start finding their way into the sticky fingers of every crook on her payroll instead of into the cash boxes where they belonged. She was about to nail a ticket jock who she suspected of doing business using the classic five-for-you-and-one-for-me routine when the sight of a teenage girl stuffing popcorn into her mouth stopped her dead. With so much on her mind, Olga had completely forgotten about keeping the nurse fed while she was locked up in the cellar. There was no need to wine and dine the young thing, but she had to have enough food and water to keep her from losing the fine figure that Lester had every right to expect for his money.

Olga hurried into the crowded bingo tent, cooking up a story to explain a short absence. "Jocko," she growled at a one-armed number caller who had managed to avoid being fired longer than anyone else on the lot, "I'm heading over to my trailer to do some paperwork. Tell anyone you see headed that way that they better think twice before bothering me. You got that?"

"Aye, aye, Boss Lady."

Olga had never decided if Jocko was giving her a hard time when he talked like that. If she ever made up her mind that he was, he was going to get decked; she didn't care how many arms he was missing. In the meantime, she was free to do what she had to do. After grabbing an armload of Cracker Jack boxes and a six-pack of bottled water from the storage closet in her trailer, Olga ducked into the dark woods behind the lot. She stumbled on a root and snagged her jeans on the thorns of an invisible bush but knew better than to turn on the flashlight until the bright lights of the carnival disappeared behind her.

11

To Patricia Dugan, Wednesdays were an island that was too far away from the last weekend and not close enough to the next one. Not that she ever did anything exciting on weekends, or on any other day of the week for that matter. She tried to sweep away such a depressing reminder as she pushed her computer cart into the nurses' station, made one final note about medications for the patient in Room 314, and sat wearily next to her friend Rita Anselmo.

"Tough day?" Rita asked, emptying a plastic jigger of half-and-half into her coffee.

Patricia shrugged. "Long but okay. The computer notes are up to date. Mrs. Sanders in 328 keeps asking for her son, Leon, but there is no one but a sister in Baltimore listed on her profile. I left a message with patient services."

"That's so sad. The last time anyone in my family was in the hospital, their room looked like the monthly meeting of the Hargrove Italian-American Club." Rita tried the coffee and made a face. "Yuk. How old is this stuff?"

Patricia laughed. "I'll make a fresh pot before I leave."

"You go home. The mighty second shift is here!"

Rita shook her head as Patricia stood and stretched. "Look at you. After a twelve-hour shift, you still look like a beautiful Irish princess. Me, I'll look like Rita the Washer Woman by the time I go home."

"You will not, and you know it."

The two friends were different in every way imaginable. Patricia Dugan had been born with beautiful chestnut hair and pearl-white skin, gifts from two sets of Irish grandparents. Rita, the taller of the two, had hair as black as nature could manage and the olive skin typical of her big Sicilian family. Except when she was around the few people she knew and trusted, Patricia said very little. Rita entered a room like a small parade. Her vivid descriptions of the Anselmo family's home life fascinated Patricia, who had been an only child, and made her more than a little envious. Patricia had never met any of her friend's family, but she knew from Rita's stories that she had two brothers, a "perfectly overweight" mother, a father who looked like a character out of *The Godfather*, and three grandparents who lived with them. By all accounts, the family's favorite pastime was sitting around the dining room table and eating. Being part of such a family, Patricia often imagined, would have been like traveling to a world where she had never been.

Rita scrolled the computer screen, studying the list of patients she was inheriting. She said, "Hmm" a couple of times and "Okay, that makes sense" once, nodded, and looked up at Patricia. "You run along. I've got this."

Patricia didn't especially want to run along. There was nothing waiting for her at the apartment she shared with two roommates. One, a second-grade teacher, would be at the singles bar where she practically lived, and the other would be locked in her bedroom typing away on the historical romance that was going to end her life as a waitress and bring her fame and fortune. The thought of hugs and pasta at the end of a long day caused her to look at Rita with envy that she did her best to disguise with a smile.

It wasn't until the elevator doors opened downstairs in the main lobby that Patricia remembered she had meant to talk to Mrs. Banakowski before she left the hospital. After the other two passengers nodded goodnight, she pushed the third-floor button and watched nervously as the doors slid closed. Ever since she was a little girl, confinement of any type, even a short ride in an elevator, took her breath away. She closed her eyes and pictured the wide-open field covered with long, green grass into which her mind had learned to flee whenever she was the prisoner of closed doors or rooms without windows. The trip back to the third floor was over before she had a chance to look for the white horses that sometimes grazed on the far side of her imaginary field.

Mary Beth waved Patricia into her office and pointed to a chair in front of her desk.

"Yes, Doctor," Mary Beth said into the telephone tucked against her shoulder, "I knew she was your daughter when I interviewed her."

Mary Beth listened, rolling her eyes. "But being a registered nurse is a prerequisite for that position."

Patricia was embarrassed to be listening to a conversation that was none of her business, and the fact that she could only hear half of it did not make her feel any more comfortable. She started to get up and wait in the empty outer office when Mary Beth tapped on her desk and pointed Patricia back into her chair.

"I know that she graduated from the University of Pennsylvania. Penn is an excellent school, but her degree is in East Asian languages and civilizations."

She looked across the desk, signaling with a raised finger that she would not be much longer. "I'm sure that you know many people on the hospital's board of directors." She held the telephone at arm's length and stared at it for a few seconds before clicking it off and placing it on her desk. "He never even said goodbye," she said, smiling warmly at Patricia. "Aren't you supposed to be on your way home by now?"

"I just handed off my patients to Rita, but before I left, I wanted to remind you that I won't be in until noon tomorrow."

Mary Beth turned to her computer, tapped the keyboard expertly, studied the screen, and tapped again. "Got it. I have Kelly filling in for you until one just in case you run a little late."

"Thank you, Mrs. Banakowski."

"If you don't start calling me Mary Beth, I'm going to start calling you Miss Dugan. How would you like that?"

Patricia's face flushed. "Yes, Ma'am. I mean, no, Ma'am. It's just…"

"I'm kidding you, Patricia. Enjoy your half-day off tomorrow."

"Thank you, but it's not that kind of day off." Patricia stood, glanced toward the empty door, and lowered her voice. "I have to go up to that place in Baltimore that puts the inserts in my shoe. My back has been bothering me. Not too badly," she quickly added, "but I want to see if they can do something before it does become a problem."

Mary Beth leaned back in her chair and studied the young nurse. In her position, she was not supposed to have favorites, but over the years, she had learned that when dealing with human beings, avoiding attachments was simply not possible. She had not been around to hold Patricia's hand when she took her first uncertain steps or to help her with her spelling homework, but she had been the one who hired her fresh out of nursing school and watched her grow in the confidence and skills required to care for and comfort patients within the demanding, and sometimes exasperating, structure of a busy hospital like Saint Joe's. Mary Beth was also the only person who knew that, as the result of serious injuries suffered in an automobile accident when she was only eight years old, this beautiful young woman had been left with a left leg that was slightly shorter than her right leg. She was also the only one at the hospital except for Rita Anselmo who knew that both of Patricia Dugan's parents had been killed in the same accident.

"I'll be fine," Patricia assured Mary Beth. "The last time this happened, they only had to make a slight adjustment to the orthotic and the problem went away."

"I'm sure you will be." If she had not been afraid of embarrassing such a shy person, Mary Beth would have come out from behind her desk and given Patricia the kind of hug she had probably not had since her mother and father died.

The overhead light inside Patricia's car faded in slow motion when she closed the door and pulled the seatbelt across her waist. She studied the gas gauge, remembering that she had to drive to Baltimore in the morning. The tank was more than half full. She did the math in her head and decided she could drive to Baltimore and back three times before the needle touched "E." Three blocks from the hospital parking lot she changed her mind and pulled into a Shell station. *Gas gauges aren't perfect,* she reminded herself.

There was a twinge of pain in her back when she got out of the car and again when she slid back in. It wasn't much, not enough to cause her to walk with a limp as long as she concentrated. Tomorrow, the people at the orthopedic shoe store would carefully examine what they called her functional leg length and make a new insert. The last time she went to see them, they only had to add an eighth of an inch. That had been almost two years ago, but she still remembered what an incredible difference such a small change had made. The unmistakable limp she walked with in her bare feet had completely disappeared when she put on the new shoes.

As Patricia eased her car out of the Shell station and turned right onto Kennedy Street, the headlights following her made identical moves. When she pulled into the Panera parking lot, the headlights moved slowly past her and went dark one aisle away.

"For here or to go?" the smiling teenager behind the counter asked. Patricia answered, "To go" without thinking but quickly changed her mind. With one roommate out for the night and the other one locked in her bedroom, she would only end up eating alone back at the apartment. At least here there were people and, even if she wasn't part of it, the cozy glow of conversation.

Patricia found an empty booth, slipped the paperback copy of *Little Women* from her purse, positioned the salt and pepper shakers to hold it open, and stirred her soup as she began to read. It was a story she first read in high school, and the paperback copy in front of her was a replacement for one that had literally fallen apart. She loved imagining that she lived in the bustling March household, not as one of the sisters but somehow remaining herself, maybe as a cousin who had come to live with them and was blessed to play a part in their busy lives. She read the story in small doses, but she read it constantly, telling herself that Marmee loved her as much as she loved her daughters. From the story's well-worn pages, Patricia extracted a sense of warmth that eased the pain of losing her own family so long ago.

A handsome man smiled as he passed her booth, and as always, she resisted an uncomfortable desire to smile back. No man would want a woman with a crippled leg. Patricia truly believed that. At some point, no matter how much any man might come to like her, he would learn the truth, and there would be more sorrow in her life. She concentrated on the book without absorbing a single word and the moment passed. Sometimes they said hello, and she was forced to rudely ignore them. One devastating crash was enough for one lifetime. She had never confessed to Rita that the reason she could not come to dinner with her family was the fear that one of her brothers would take an interest in her without knowing that in the end, he would discover that she was a cripple.

Olga stood outside the restaurant's glass wall and studied the young nurse, satisfied that Lester Turner was going to be extremely happy with the perfection of his new toy. Almost as happy as she was going to be with a boatload of his money.

There was no reason for her to stand around in the dark, waiting. Olga knew exactly what the girl was going to do next. She would park on the narrow street behind the Greengate Apartments and use a footpath through the complex to reach the entrance to Building Number One where she lived. Halfway along that path, the low-hanging branches of a weeping willow formed a pitch-black tunnel where like a spider in a carefully spun web, Olga would be waiting.

12

T.J. Barnes pulled into the long driveway with the fine-trimmed lawn, amazed as always by the size of the houses in the gated subdivision where Mary Beth lived. He had no idea how much money her late husband, Wade Banakowski, had piled up running the biggest insurance agency in Maryland, but he assumed it was more than a police chief would make in a hundred years. Closing the door of his cruiser, he studied the stone-faced structure directly across the street, trying to decide if it would be considered a mansion or just a ridiculously large house with four garage doors and a fountain in the front yard big enough to swim in.

He turned, took a breath, and told himself the same thing he had been telling himself the entire way over: *Just relax and be yourself. This woman you are about to have dinner with is the same girl you took to the senior prom when her name was Mary Beth Conner and she lived in the same kind of house that everyone else lived in. In fact,* he reassured himself, *no matter what happens, tonight will be a hell of a lot easier to deal with than the first time he got up the nerve to ask her out.* There would be no interrogation by her suspicious father, no icy stares from her protective mother, and no bared-fangs hissing by a green-eyed cat that never did warm up to him. Every bit of that reassurance evaporated when he came face to face with a carved oak door that looked like the entrance to a castle. Staring at an ivory doorbell and a heavy brass knocker shaped like a horseshoe, T.J. wondered if the choice he had to make was a test, like using the correct fork or knowing which bread plate was his. He took a stab and rang the bell.

With a phone pressed to her ear, Mary Beth opened the door and waved him inside. "Has anyone heard anything from her?" she asked into the phone before staring up at the ceiling and listening.

"This is not like her at all," she interrupted. "I haven't been able to reach her on her cellphone, and no one answers the number at the apartment where she lives. Her roommates are probably at work." Again she listened, walking slowly away from T.J. and leaning against an arched doorframe separating the marble-floored foyer from a high-ceilinged room lined with bookshelves.

Still listening, Mary Beth looked at T.J. "I have every intention of informing them. As a matter of fact, the police have just arrived at my house. And Rita, call me right away if you hear from her."

She walked slowly into the book-filled room and placed the phone in its cradle. "T.J., one of my nurses didn't show up for work today," she said without turning around.

He would have reminded Mary Beth that people miss work every day if it had not been for the unmistakable alarm that underlined her words. "The nurse you are talking about," he asked, changing gears, "has she ever missed work before?"

"Not without telling me ahead of time. She was scheduled to have the morning off but she was due back right after lunch." Mary Beth sat down and stared at the phone. "This is completely unlike Patricia."

"Patricia?"

"Patricia Dugan."

T.J. had learned from experience that the reasons adults went missing would fill an entire chapter of a police textbook. Many of them reappeared later the same day with perfectly legitimate explanations like appointments they had forgotten to tell anyone about or sudden urges to spend the day shopping or jump in the car and take off for the beach. Others he dealt with had dropped out of sight for more serious reasons like drug addiction or to flee a mountain of debt too overwhelming to handle. There was domestic abuse, dementia, and the lure of green grass on the other side of fences that didn't exist. At the tragic end of the list were suicides and abductions, and once in his career, a car that ran off a road in a rural part of the county and remained undiscovered for the better part of two months. It was the old story of hoping for the best and being prepared for the worst, and because of that, T.J. had learned to walk into these situations one careful step at a time.

He crossed his arms and leaned against the doorframe. "Tell me about her, Mary Beth. I heard you mention roommates. Do you know if her parents are living or if she has any siblings?"

Mary Beth shook her head. "No brothers or sisters. Her parents were killed when she was a young girl."

The nervous anticipation of a dinner date vanished as T.J. trained his sights on the type of situation he had dealt with many times. "Any close friends you know of?" he asked. "A boyfriend?"

"I don't think there was a boyfriend. She was so sweet and shy." Horrified that she had used the word *was*, Mary Beth stood up, marched into the foyer, and pulled open the front door.

"T.J., take me to her apartment. I wrote down the address before I left the hospital."

There were moments like these when it seemed like they had never been apart. "The Bulldog," he used to call her when she decided there was something that had to be done and that she was the one who was going to do it. The narrowed eyes, the look that said, *Come with me or get out of my way*, were so familiar that for a moment, T.J. was speechless.

"Come on, come on," she said, pushing him toward the door. "We have a missing nurse to find."

T.J. could not help smiling. "Okay, Bulldog, let's go get 'em."

Mary Beth punched him on the shoulder. Hard. It hurt. He had forgotten how mad she got when he called her Bulldog. What he had not forgotten was that if one of her nurses, or anyone else she cared about, was in trouble, they could not have a better friend in their corner than the woman pulling him toward his police car.

"Aren't you going to turn on the lights and siren?" Mary Beth asked as they pulled out of her driveway.

Without thinking, T.J. reached over and patted her knee. "We're good. It won't take very long to get to that address." What had been an instinctive reassuring gesture set off an explosion of old feelings that startled him. *You are a fifty-six-year-old man,* he lectured himself, *so stop thinking like an idiot.* The little talking-to unraveled in confusion when she took his hand into hers and squeezed it.

"I hope not," she answered. "I'm worried sick."

Except for the punch in the shoulder, this was the first time she had touched him in so long that it seemed like forever. He wondered if she would suddenly realize what she was doing and let go, but all she did was peer through the windshield into the night. "Not to be a backseat driver," she asked, "but shouldn't you have turned right back there and cut across Baltimore Road?"

"Trust me. I know every shortcut in Hargrove County."

Of course he would, Mary Beth reminded herself, embarrassed that she had asked such a dumb question. Anybody who had been on the police force as long as T.J. would know the county the way most people knew their way around the block.

He made a sharp turn onto a road she never used and flipped on the cruiser's flashing lights long enough to pass a slow-moving truck.

"Patricia Dugan," he said aloud, swinging back into his lane. "How old is she?"

Mary Beth answered twenty-four.

"And you said there is no boyfriend that you know about?"

"That isn't the kind of thing the nurses discuss with me, but my guess would be no."

"And why is that?"

"Just a feeling I have. Patricia is so quiet and shy, and—I don't know—she seems even younger in some ways than she is."

T.J. hit the flashing lights again when they came to a four-way stop sign. He looked both ways without coming to a stop. "How about a best friend?"

"I don't know about friends outside of the hospital,

but she and another nurse named Rita Anselmo are very close."

"Rita Anselmo? Isn't that the nurse I met in your office?"

"That's right, you did. You told her you knew her father, Vito."

"Right, Big Vito. What can you tell me about her?"

"She's an excellent nurse, just like Patricia, but personality-wise, the two of them are like night and day. Rita has a big, Italian-American personality just like everyone else in her family."

"You know Rita's family?"

"They live in that enormous stone house right across the street from me, the one with the big fountain. Good people. Ever since Wade died, Vito sends his men over to cut my grass and rake the leaves. They even shovel the driveway when it snows. God bless him."

T.J. asked the questions thoughtfully with spaces between them that he filled silently with an experienced evaluation of each answer. The boyish uncertainty that made it impossible for him to ask a girl he had known since high school out to dinner disappeared the second he strapped himself into a police car. The change did not surprise Mary Beth. The T.J. she knew had always been like that, focused and tough when there was a job to be done or a football game to be played but completely useless when it came to asking a girl to the prom or manning up on her front porch when a goodnight kiss was his for the taking.

"Finally, I know where we are," Mary Beth said, distracted by something about the shape of the passing darkness. "Aren't we near that old church that folded after its pastor ran off with all the money?"

"With every last cent and an attractive widow who played the organ," T.J. filled in. "It's over there in the dark somewhere, vacant and falling apart."

"I can't see it," Mary Beth said, staring. "But what are all those lights in the trees over there?"

T.J. slowed to see what she was talking about. Beads of yellow glimmered in the forest of trees surrounding the unseen church, and high above them, the top of a Ferris wheel spun red and yellow in the sky. "Those lights are not *in* the trees, they're *behind* them. That's the fireman's carnival, a major headache I didn't need."

"Has there been trouble?"

"Not really but directing carnival traffic and assigning people to keep an eye on things takes manpower I don't have."

They had just passed Michele's Florists, the lights in its leafy windows bright against the night, when suddenly, other lights, these flashing red on a railroad gate, brought their dash to Patricia's apartment to a skidding halt.

A blinding beam of light emerged from the trees at the head of a thunderous caravan of freight cars on its nightly run through the county. The ground under the police car shook as sparks showered the graveled rail bed and the locomotive's unworldly whistle blasted the night. T.J. knew from his many meetings with the railroad that this particular train, the weeknight Baltimore run, carried anywhere from ninety to 120 freight cars, that it was not supposed to exceed fifty miles per hour at the Woodyard Road grade crossing, and that even at fifty-five miles per hour, it would take at least a mile for the train to come to a stop after the engineer hit the emergency brake.

"Do these trains always go this fast?" a startled Mary Beth asked.

"They're not supposed to but they do," T.J. answered with more feeling than he intended. "We were monitoring the nightly speeds until I had to pull the officer who was doing it and assign him to the carnival."

"I didn't know trains were your responsibility."

"They are if I care about people getting killed at this crossing."

The caboose clattered through the crossing, leaving the nighttime crickets too startled to get back to work. "Can you imagine what would happen if somebody tried to drive around that gate to save a few minutes?" he asked quietly.

If T.J. had been a different kind of man, he would have answered his own question by sharing the sickening details of an accident where a van had pulled out in front of a semi because its driver was running late on a delivery. And that was a Mack Truck, not a locomotive, he reminded himself. In his long career, T.J. had never seen what a freight train would do to the car or van of an impatient driver, and he hoped he never would.

"All right, let's go," he said, looking both ways twice before crossing the tracks. "We have a nurse to find."

T.J. was confident they would do just that. Every missing persons statistic he had ever read was heavily weighted in favor of someone like Patricia Dugan turning up unharmed. It was entirely possible that she would show up for her shift at the hospital tomorrow, embarrassed and apologetic that she had not called to explain that some sort of problem had come up unexpectedly. Whatever it turned out to be might even seem funny after everybody took a deep breath and relaxed. He was about to tell the story of a young schoolteacher who, as unbelievable as it sounded, had neglected to tell anyone that she was taking a seven-day cruise out of Baltimore when he saw that Mary Beth was wiping tears from her eyes.

"It's going to be fine," T.J. assured her as the railroad crossing and the dark road behind them slipped into the night.

Right before the train stopped them, Mary Beth had experienced the strangest feeling that they were near Patricia. She studied the dark night, but all she could see were the distant carnival lights. She had started to say something, but in the deafening racket, T.J. had not heard her. As they moved away from the crossing, the feeling grew fainter and fainter, and when it was there no more, she decided that she was so sick with worry that it was hard to think straight.

"I'm sure you're right," she answered, embarrassed to realize that she was still holding his hand.

13

Hidden in the dark night between the railroad crossing and the shimmering carnival lights, the old church trembled in the violence of the nightly freight train. A forgotten hymnal worked its way to the edge of a shaking pew and tumbled to the dusty floor, an indiscretion unnoticed by the terrified captive in the cellar below or the woman who had slapped her awake and stripped her bare.

"Stay calm, Sweetie," Olga said with the indifference of a doctor, "I just want to take a good look at the goods."

Patricia Dugan was too stunned to scream. If she had been able to think straight, she might have remembered walking from the car to her apartment, wishing she had the nerve to accept Rita's invitations to have dinner with her family, when hands as hard as steel seized her by the neck. There was an explosion of pain, confused dreams, and the humiliation of finding herself completely naked in front of a woman whose penetrating eyes swept over her like probing fingers.

"Stand up and walk over to those stairs, then turn around and walk back to me," Olga ordered, rolling Patricia's nursing uniform into a ball and tossing it into the mocking shadows.

Patricia had trouble understanding the woman. Pain shot through her back and neck when she tried to sit up. Turning against the pain, she saw a rusted boiler that, in the deep shadows cast by a bare bulb hanging from the ceiling, looked like a many-armed monster. There was no hint of day or night, only windowless walls streaked with the filth of neglect. Panicking, Patricia closed her eyes and searched frantically for the grassy field with the white horses into which she always fled when she found herself trapped.

"Don't make me say it again," Olga commanded, grabbing Patricia by the arm and yanking her off the rotted cot. "Over to the stair and back! Move!"

Too terrified to notice, Patricia fouled herself.

"That's disgusting," Olga swore, shoving her captive toward the stair. "Move!"

Patricia steadied herself as best she could and took a few uncertain steps. Confusion, fear, and pain did nothing to numb the shameful experience of being naked in front of a stranger. Except for when she was a little girl, she had never been naked in front of anyone. Even at the doctor's office, they gave her one of those cotton gowns to cover everything the doctor didn't need to see.

"Walk right!" a confused Olga screamed as the girl limped, sobbing, toward the stairs. Patricia needed to go to the bathroom again and didn't know what to do.

Olga moved closer, assuming that the shadowy light was playing tricks on her eyes. "Turn around and walk toward me," she demanded.

Patricia couldn't do it. It had been mortifying enough to be naked with her back turned. Turning around would be like surrendering completely.

"Turn around and walk toward me!" Olga screamed, and this time, power unlike anything Patricia had ever experienced in another human caused her to turn like a robot, close her eyes against the shame of showing herself, and move unsteadily toward the monster of this nightmare. A monster she knew she had seen somewhere before.

"You have a gimp leg! You little bitch, you have a gimp leg!" Olga shoved Patricia to the floor and ran her hands and eyes along the pleading girl's legs. In disbelief, Olga yanked Patricia up by the hair and slammed her against the wall. "You think Lester's going to pay all that money for a woman with a gimp leg? Do you?" she screamed.

Patricia was too frozen with fear to speak. She tried to drop to her knees and pray but Olga locked her powerful arms around Patricia's neck. "You wasted my time, Girl!" she hissed as she squeezed with every ounce of her strength. There were no referees to stop her.

Olga awoke and stared up at the small, sun-filled window of her trailer, half-remembering a dream in which Lester Turner was laughing his head off about the way a young nurse with a bad leg had made a fool of her. She pushed herself from the mattress and stared into the late morning brightness. Through the folded flaps of the bingo tent, she watched her huddled crew jump-start their day with coffee and cigarettes and a bottle in a paper bag. She couldn't wait to get rid of every last one of them.

"Goddamn it!" she swore, slamming her open palm against the wall so hard that the trailer rocked like a boat. Olga had never in her career been pinned, not even when the script called for it. More than one smug beast had been dumbfounded when she shoved her aside at the count of two and nailed her ass to the canvas. "If you want to do something about it," she loved to whisper in their ears, "I'll be in the locker room."

It wasn't until she opened a bottle of water and splashed her face that Olga was jolted with the realization that the game was far from over. Every muscle in her body came alive. "How dumb are you?" she tore into herself, hunting for her shoes. "How could you possibly forget that first morning in the diner?" She almost exploded with excitement thinking about it. "There were two pretty nurses. Not one. Two!" She even remembered the name of the second one. Rita. Almost humming, which might have been a first, Olga calculated the chances of both nurses being crippled. She would check to make sure when she got her hands on the pretty Italian one, but she was willing to bet a Cadillac Eldorado she did not yet own that the chance of something like that happening was less than zero.

14

The window curtains remained tightly drawn at Lester Turner's mansion high above Lake Michigan. A heavy Baroque gate at the end of the oak-lined driveway opened only to those recognized by a security system with sophistication unimaginable in the days when the sprawling estate was built by Lester's grandfather. Day and night, the eyes and ears of the same system scanned the grounds for uninvited visitors and unlikely escapees.

Until the night Lester began to wonder if painted eyes were capable of witnessing the unholy performances taking place there, the mansion's high-ceilinged library had been dominated by a monarch-size oil painting of The Ball Bearing King himself, Simpson L. Turner. For the same irrational reason, a portrait of Lester's father, Simpson L. Jr., had lost its honored position above the fireplace in the formal dining room. The two portraits, shrouded in dust cloths, remained in the mansion's vast basement until it occurred to Lester that their masterfully painted ears might well be capable of detecting the lewd cheers that frequently filled the rooms above them.

Lester took no more interest in the family ball bearing empire than he had taken in the three ivy-covered universities where he was briefly enrolled. He loved fast cars and willing women and understood early that possessing piles of money facilitated the enjoyment of both. Spending time at the company's corporate headquarters in Chicago, even if he never did anything resembling work, proved to be an annoying complication. The only reason he showed up was because his father, who inherited the business from his grandfather, threatened to cut him off without a dime if he didn't. By a happy circumstance, this annoying complication disappeared from Lester's life when his father, who was in the habit of enjoying late-night strolls on the mansion grounds, inexplicably lost his way in the dark and fell to his death from a cliff high above the lake.

Against the advice of his board of directors and the numerous financial advisers employed by his late father, Lester sold the privately held company to a consortium of Japanese businesses and made the pursuit of pleasure his full-time occupation. He was twenty-eight years old at the time.

The solitary gardener who tended the grounds for Lester had never set foot inside the main house and rarely spoke to the ancient housekeeper who clearly understood that her very generous salary and comfortable living quarters were rewards for her willingness to see nothing and hear nothing.

In the years that followed his father's death, Lester oversaw the construction of a six-car garage and, more recently, the conversion of a large room above the garage into what he described to the contractor as a Middle East veneration chamber. The term meant nothing but it answered any questions the contractor or his workers had about such things as the raised padded platform in the middle of the room, the carefully placed mirrors, and the fact that the only access to the space was from Lester's adjacent bedroom.

It was into this chamber of pleasure that Lester strolled the day after his most recent telephone conversation with Olga. Excited as a small boy who had been promised a new toy, he played with the dimmer system that controlled a network of recessed light fixtures and tested the concealed video system. He sat on the satin-sheeted platform, bounced on it, laid on it, and laughed into the crystal mirror above the bed. What had Olga told him, "A young nurse, unspoiled and perfect in every way?" The anticipation of having his way with such a creature however and whenever he wanted, and the unchecked joy of sharing her with his special friends, was almost more than he could stand.

Downstairs in the garage, the van was ready, ingeniously disguised as an ambulance as it waited among the Porches, Bentleys, and Lamborghinis, fully fueled and ready for the run down to Maryland. Like the playroom, the van had been specially equipped to keep Lester's latest acquisition comfortable but completely under control. "It's going to be a surprise donation to the fire department," Lester explained to his mechanic as the man installed a cot equipped with arm and leg straps and a portable toilet. At Lester's request, the mechanic bolted brackets to the underside of the passenger seat, not for the first aid kit he described but for a large valise that would be stuffed with money. Twice, as he awaited Olga's next call, Lester fell asleep in the van, dreaming the most wonderful dreams.

15

If Olga needed any reminders about the ways Lester's money could change her life, she got one in the diner parking lot when she pulled into a space next to the car of her dreams. She slammed the Bronco's dented door and pressed her face against the window of a silver Cadillac Eldorado that was as long as a boat. It was all there: the pleated leather seats, the polished wood steering wheel, and enough buttons and knobs to fly an airplane. More than anything in the world, she wanted to sink into a seat like that, take command of those controls, and leave the carnival world far behind. "You piece of shit," she hissed at the Bronco with anger fueled by the maddening reality of how close she had been to calling Lester and telling him to get his ass down here with the money. She forced herself to stop drooling over the Eldorado and stomped into the diner. The surprise she had gotten in the church cellar had knocked Olga off balance, but that was all it had done. She was back on her feet, ready to climb back into the ring, and starving.

She checked the menu board. A number seven with black coffee looked like just the thing.

"English muffin or biscuit with that?"

"Muffin. Make it two."

"One Belly Buster, double muffs," Sissy Wagner called over her shoulder while pouring Olga's coffee. "We met the morning you were meeting with the county council about your carnival. I remember talking to you."

Olga, lost in the details of a revised plan for getting her hands on Lester's money, managed a nod.

"Anyway, I saw that your carnival opened, so I guess the meeting went okay," Sissy persisted. In her business, she had learned that a lot of people had trouble speaking before their first jolt of coffee.

Olga managed another nod.

"I guess you heard about that poor missing nurse," Sissy tried while refilling a napkin dispenser.

The word "nurse" jolted Olga. She sensed danger, a sea of quicksand spreading before her. She emptied the cup and stared into it, measuring her words before answering. "Seems I heard something," she said carefully.

"Patricia Dugan," Sissy continued. "She came in here every morning before going to work at the hospital. Sweetest girl I ever met."

"Belly Buster up!" came the call from the kitchen window. "Double muffs!"

"As a matter of fact," Sissy remembered, sliding the steaming plate across the counter, "I think both

Patricia and her friend Rita came in for coffee the morning you were here."

Long years in the school of street smarts had educated Olga about the dangers of speaking in a hurry. She cut up a sausage and mixed it into the scrambled eggs that came with a stack of pancakes. "Don't really remember," she answered as nonchalantly as she could manage. "I had a lot on my mind that morning."

"Patricia is very pretty, reddish hair, fair skin. Rita was the one with…" Sissy stopped in mid-sentence. Her face lit up. "Speaking of the devil! How are you this morning, Rita!"

"Okay, I guess," Rita Anselmo replied quietly as she slid onto the stool next to Olga.

"That's the way to be, Honey," Sissy assured her. "Patricia is going to show up and be just fine. You wait and see."

Don't count on it, Olga cackled deep inside like the cartoon witches she had always loved.

Rita forced a smile. "All I know is that I'm saying more prayers than I have since I was a little girl." She turned to look at Olga for the first time.

Sissy attempted an introduction. "Rita Anselmo, this is the owner of the carnival everyone is talking about, but…" She hesitated. "…I'm afraid I don't know her name."

Olga Muntz had been thrown completely off balance by the unexpected appearance of the very person who was going to save the day. She managed to tell

Sissy her name and glanced at Rita long enough to confirm that Lester would not be able to keep his hands off her.

"Pleased to meet you," Rita said, making an effort to sound interested when all she could think about was Patricia. "My father wants to take me to your carnival to get my mind off..." she hesitated, trying to not think about the terrible possibilities. A sudden smile brightened her face. "Speaking of my father, next Wednesday is his birthday."

"Well, happy birthday to Big Vito," Sissy toasted with an empty coffee mug. "What are you going to get him?"

"Just a box of cannolis from Capparelli's. He doesn't let us buy him presents, but he won't get mad if it's something good to eat."

Sissy was completely surprised by the cannoli part of this news. "Has the bakery reopened?"

"Not yet," Rita answered. "Mr. Capparelli is still fighting with the insurance company, but his wife will make things at home if you call her."

Sissy noticed how intently Olga was following their conversation and assumed that was because she had no idea what they were talking about. "Capparelli's was an incredible Italian bakery," she explained, "until a telephone pole crashed through their roof when the county got hit by a hurricane last year. They've been closed ever since."

Olga didn't give a damn about bakeries or telephone poles; what she wanted to do was take a good look at the goods, the long black hair, the beautiful skin, and a body that not even loose nurses' scrubs could tone down. She noticed that this one smiled more than the other one, not that she was going to do much smiling when Lester and his friends got hold of her.

"The Capparellis are babysitting for their daughter Ursula on Wednesday night, but Mrs. Capparelli said she would leave the cannolis on the back porch for me," Rita was telling Sissy when Olga tuned back in.

On a back porch where? Olga urged silently.

Checking her watch, Rita asked for a coffee to go with one cream and two sugars.

"Coming right up," Sissy answered. "Before I forget, tell me where Mrs. Capparelli lives. I'm going to give her a call and order some of her famous biscottis."

"On Olive Street, all the way down at the end."

Wednesday night. Back porch. End of Olive Street. There was only one more thing Olga had to know. As Rita left the diner, Olga concentrated on her every step. There was not even a hint of a limp. If anything, this one moved as smoothly as an athlete.

16

The line of people waiting to ride the Ferris wheel had grown every night since the carnival opened. "See for miles from the top!" a whiskey-faced barker shouted into a megaphone. "Right this way! See halfway to Baltimore!"

There might have been a law against such blatant exaggeration, but no one was complaining. The flight of the big wheel arced above a festival of yellow lights illuminating avenues of striped arcade tents and an open-sided bingo pavilion where a numbers caller struggled to be heard above screams rising from a dozen jam-packed rides at the far end of the grounds. For thrilling seconds, as the Ferris wheel passengers reached the top, Michele's florist shop appeared and disappeared beyond a sea of nighttime treetops, followed by a phantom-like sighting of the moon-washed church steeple hiding in the woods. If the ride was perfectly timed, ticketholders were treated to a glimpse of flashing red gate lights and the tunneling beam of a freight train thundering through the night.

THE CARNIVAL

There had been rain that morning, but by evening, the skies were clear and cars were double-parked in the matted-grass parking lot, delighting Fire Chief Jerry Donnelly who was manning a raffle booth at the front gate.

"How many do you want, T.J.?" Jerry sang out, trying not to look surprised when he spotted the police chief who, for the first time in his memory, was with a woman. "Win the Little Lady that beautiful Harley," he grinned, pointing to a muscular motorcycle with streamers of colorful balloons tied to the handlebars. "Five dollars a book, six books for twenty-five dollars. What do you say?"

"Do those balloons come with it?"

"Buy six books and I'll give you a damn balloon," Jerry laughed. "And then," he added in what he considered a stroke of merchandising genius, "you can give the balloon to your lovely lady."

Having to introduce a woman was a new experience for T.J., a shortcoming so obvious that Mary Beth introduced herself.

"Did you say Banakowski?" Jerry asked.

"Yes. I think you knew my husband, Wade Banakowski. He was a big supporter of the volunteer fire department. To tell you the truth, I suspected it was his secret dream to be a fireman."

"Of course, Wade Banakowski! He was extremely generous to the department. And a very nice guy." Jerry stopped, not sure if he should be raving about

Mary Beth's late husband in front of T.J.

T.J. took out his wallet. "Six books of chances and a balloon, a blue one."

"As in police department blue?" Jerry grinned, untying a string from the motorcycle and handing it to Mary Beth.

To T.J.'s surprise, Mary Beth had called him from the hospital and asked if he would take her to the carnival. "It probably won't do much good," she admitted, "but if I don't do something, I'm going to go crazy worrying about Patricia."

"As long as you don't mind riding in a police car again," he had answered. "I'm going there on business. I may buy some popcorn and throw a few baseballs at wooden milk bottles while I'm at it, but after what happened two years ago, I want to see for myself how things are going."

To keep an eye on things, T.J. assigned officers to patrol the carnival in plain clothes. There had been only one arrest. Larry Baker, who joined the force after growing tired of teaching high school English, watched a woman put a purse on the ground while she lifted her two children into the miniature airplane ride. His report stated that he was debating whether he should tell her to be more careful with her purse when a man he described as looking like a painter grabbed it and stuck it under his shirt.

"A painter?" T.J. asked the young officer when he read the report. "You mean like an artist?"

"No, sir, a house kind of painter. You know, white pants and white shirt with different colors spilled all over them." To the surprise of no one familiar with police station humor, his report earned him the nickname "Rembrandt," a good-natured rib that Private Baker seemed to like.

It was Corporal Nick Suit's turn to work undercover, but T.J. had yet to spot him. While he continued to look, he bought a box of popcorn and handed it to Mary Beth.

"Have you contacted the FBI about Patricia?" she asked.

"I'll do that the minute we have evidence that it was in fact a kidnapping."

"Evidence? Like what?"

"Like a ransom demand, for one thing. It's an over-simplification, but all we know right now is that Patricia Dugan is a missing adult." T.J. caught himself about to cite a statistic stating that at any given moment, there were ninety thousand missing adults in the United States, a nugget of information that had always astounded him.

Mary Beth tried not to show her frustration with T.J.'s businesslike answer. He knew what he was doing, she was sure of that, but he seemed so calm and methodical about the whole thing that she was ready to scream.

"I told you that Sergeant Jenkins interviewed Patricia's two roommates again, didn't I?" T.J. asked. "The only thing he learned was that the two of them are so freaked out about Patricia's disappearance that they're moving back home with their parents." He continued to look for Corporal Suit while they made their way through the crowd. "Let me see, what else? We located her car on the side street near her apartment where her roommates said she always parked. There was no sign of a struggle, and the only fingerprints we found in the car were Patricia's."

He stopped, finding it strange that he had not spotted his undercover officer. "Oh, yes," he added distractedly, "there was a copy of *Little Women* in the car. The roommates said it was hers."

Mary Beth felt her eyes filling. "That story fascinated her," she said with difficulty. "If you ever read it, you might guess why."

To avoid confessing that he had read *Little Women* in high school but couldn't remember what it was about, T.J. changed the subject. "I went up to Baltimore yesterday to check out the place where Patricia was supposed to have her orthopedic shoe adjusted."

"And?"

"The manager told me she was a no-show and never called to cancel the appointment."

Mary Beth reached for his hand. "It was sweet of you to drive all the way up there yourself," she said softly. T.J. assumed that he was supposed to return the squeeze. He did but was too embarrassed to look at her at the same time.

"Evening, Chief."

Even though there was nothing in the sky brighter than a fading moon, the longhaired man who slipped up beside T.J. was wearing sunglasses. "Everything is smooth so far," he reported out of the side of his mouth. "Those crazy women with the yellow tee shirts are still in the parking lot handing out fliers about the evils of carnivals." He nudged T.J. and slipped him a piece of folded paper. "I saved you one."

T.J. was confused but only for a minute. Neither the wig nor the sunglasses could disguise the shit-eating grin he knew so well. "Corporal Suit, is that you?"

"Pretty good disguise, don't you think?" With another flash of his famous smile, Nick Suit slipped back into the crowd.

You've got them well trained," Mary Beth laughed, letting go of his hand so she could shake the last of the popcorn out of the box.

"I can't take credit for that crazy costume, but I have to admit I'm impressed." He took a long look around. "I haven't seen the woman who owns this carnival."

"What does she look like?"

"Like the female wrestler she apparently was," T.J. answered, continuing to look for Olga. "Walk with me through the bingo tent and over to the rides, and then we can leave."

"I'm in no hurry," Mary Beth answered. "There's nothing for me to do at home but worry about Patricia."

"Maybe some cotton candy will help."

"I don't know. I think it's terrible for your teeth."

"How can it be? It was invented by a dentist.'

"You have to be kidding."

"Swear to God. There was an article about him in a magazine at the barbershop."

Mary Beth laughed. "In that case, I'll take some." She was trying to wrap the balloon string around her wrist when it slipped, launching the shimmering blue ball into the night sky.

"That was really cool, Mrs. Banakowski!" a delighted voice exclaimed. "I loved letting balloons go when I was a little girl."

"Rita!"

The two nurses hugged like they hadn't seen each other for months.

"T.J., this is Rita Anselmo. I think you met her in my office…"

"I remember. Big Vito is your father."

Rita's pretty face lit up. "This is him!"

A man bigger than T.J. extended a bear paw hand. "T.J. Barnes. I see you around all the time, but this is the first time we've met since I don't know when."

"Penn State at Maryland. Do you remember the score?"

"Like it was yesterday."

The two men laughed, one of them polite enough to leave it at that and the other one impressed that he had.

T.J. and Vito followed the women into a sawdust-covered avenue of tents stocked with stuffed animals and plastic prizes. Up ahead of them, Rita stopped and said something to Mary Beth who pulled her close and held her in her arms. When they started walking again, Vito put a heavy hand on T.J.'s shoulder. "I'm not kidding, Barnes," he said slowly. "If anyone ever lays a hand on my daughter, they better hope that you get to them before I do."

On television, the police officer's line would go something like "Don't do anything stupid, Vito. Let the law take care of it."

But they weren't on television, Big Vito Anselmo was no actor, and T.J. had been around long enough to know that sometimes the best thing to say is nothing.

From the small window of her trailer at the edge of the woods, Olga Muntz watched closely as Rita and Mary Beth waited for the two men to catch up with them. She might have lost the first round, but the bell was about to ring again, and she was not going to make the same mistake twice. She spread the soiled curtain with her strong fingers and concentrated on Rita's every step. "Perfect. Perfect. A few more steps, sweetheart," she whispered. "Absolutely perfect!" She let the curtain drop, sat down on her unmade cot, and dialed Lester Turner's number.

"Olga, my dear girl, how timely your telephone call is. Just last night, a small circle of my most intimate friends asked when they might assist me in welcoming my latest playmate to her new home."

"She's as good as in the bag."

"Marvelous, my dear, marvelous."

"Two hundred and fifty thousand dollars. Cash," Olga enunciated.

"My good woman, must you speak of money while visions of nubile innocence dance through my head?"

Olga Muntz returned to the window after hanging up. Nurse Number Two had disappeared into the crowd, but that was not a problem. She would be easy enough to find again.

17

If T.J. Barnes had accepted every invitation that crossed his desk, he would have spent all his time attending lunches and dinners and tasting pies at the county fair. It was all part of the job, he understood that, but it was all so time-consuming, especially when on top of everything else, there was a missing girl to be found and a carnival to keep an eye on.

When he did find himself in front of a microphone, he had but one message: Laws, big and small, were a community's way of maintaining peace and safety and providing the right kind of place for kids to grow up. T.J. didn't care how corny those words sounded. Enforcing the law was what he had signed up for when he joined the police force, and respect for the law was the platform he had run on the five times he had been elected police chief, an accomplishment every member of the county council secretly envied. He did his best to temper his respect for the law with a spoonful of reality by not firing up the siren every time he saw someone toss an empty coffee cup from a car window or roll slowly through a stop sign. This uneasy compromise was what kept him from reaching for his ticket book when he pulled up to the hospital entrance and found an Anselmo Construction Company truck parked in the fire lane.

Inside the bright orange construction fencing outlining the plaza project, a dozen workers huddled around Vito Anselmo like a football team ready to take the field. "Now let's get moving," Vito boomed. "We're pouring concrete next week, and there is a hell of a lot of work to get done between now and then!"

"I almost expected them to clap hands when they broke the huddle," T.J. said when Vito was finished.

Vito laughed. "They're a good bunch, but we have to get moving on this project. That damn mud hole over there set us back at least a week."

"The underground spring?"

"Yeah, but I think we finally got it capped."

Vito removed his hard hat and wiped his brow with the forearm of a linebacker. "What brings the police chief to the hospital this morning?" he asked.

"As a matter of fact, I'm here to talk to your daughter."

"About that poor nurse who disappeared?"

T.J. nodded.

"Had any luck finding her?"

T.J. shook his head. "I wish I could say yes, but all we can do right now is go back to the beginning and turn over the same rocks. Maybe Rita can tell us something new about the last day they worked together."

"Take it easy on her, will you? She's worried sick about that poor girl Patricia as it is."

"Did you ever meet her?" T.J. asked as they walked together toward the illegally parked truck.

Vito shook his head. "Rita talked about her once in a while; about how she had no family and all that. The whole thing is a goddamned shame."

Vito opened the door of the truck and climbed in. "I got a bad feeling about this business, and I'm sure you do too," he said as he hit the starter. "If it was my daughter, I'd be so damned mad that I'd want to break somebody's neck."

It didn't seem like the right moment for T.J. to remind the man not to park in a fire lane.

Upstairs, Rita Anselmo was wearing a Baltimore Orioles jacket over her scrubs. The word *Slugger* was embroidered above the Oriole Bird.

"Like it?" she asked, spinning around like a model. "It's a birthday present from my father."

"Happy birthday!" T.J. smiled.

"Not me, my father's. He gives all of us presents on *his* birthday, but he won't let us get him anything." She spun again, obviously delighted with the new orange-and-black jacket. "See how big it is on me? I wanted it to look like it belonged to a real Oriole."

"Rita told me that 'Slugger' is what her father called her when she played softball," Mary Beth informed T.J. from behind her desk.

"My brothers will never admit it, but I was a better hitter than either one of them," Rita laughed.

"Can I stay here and update this patient roster, or do you need privacy while you speak with Rita?" Mary Beth asked T.J. without taking her eyes from the computer screen.

"You're fine," T.J. answered. "In fact, I need both of you to think hard. Is there anything, anything at all, about the day Patricia Dugan disappeared or the days leading up to it that you might have forgotten to tell us?"

Rita's cheerfulness evaporated at the mention of Patricia's name. She fought back tears as she sat down. "I just keep thinking about how I always wanted her to come to our house and have dinner with us, and she never did."

Mary Beth pulled a tissue from the box on her desk and walked it over to Rita.

"I hoped and prayed that one of my brothers would like her, and maybe something would, you know, happen," Rita continued when she was able. "Patricia was so beautiful."

"No one was nicer to Patricia than you were," Mary Beth consoled her.

As gently as he could, T.J. went through a checklist of questions, then thanked them for bearing with him. He was about to leave when Mary Beth stopped him. "Rita, will you excuse us? I need to have a word with Mr. Police Chief." Rita took another tissue and nodded. "Love your new jacket," Mary Beth called after her.

There was something in Mary Beth's tone that made T.J. feel like he was being called to the principal's office, an experience that had been a regular feature of his school years. She marched back to her desk and motioned for T.J. to take a seat. "Thomas Jefferson Barnes," she began, "I want to make sure you do not have the misguided idea that our little stroll through the carnival the other night qualifies as the date you have been trying to get up the nerve to ask me out on."

T.J. was as tongue-tied as he had ever been in the presence of Mrs. Huffer, the legendary principal of Hargrove Elementary School. He didn't know if he was supposed to answer or keep listening.

"Because if you do," Mary Beth continued, "if you think that feeding me popcorn and cotton candy and buying me a balloon gets you off the hook, you have another think coming."

The truth was that T.J. did think that their night at the carnival had been a date. It was true that he had to go to the carnival anyway to keep an eye on things, but he had also called her up, picked her up, and brought her back home, and as best he could remember, those were all things people did on a date.

"So here is the deal," Mary Beth went on while he debated whether it would be a good idea to say any of that out loud. "My house, your house, or the country club?"

"What country club?"

"Terrapin Creek Country Club. I meant to cancel the membership when Wade died but never got around to it."

"I don't like country clubs."

"Have you ever been to one?"

"Once or twice when I couldn't get out of it."

"Okay, if Terrapin Creek is out, that leaves my house or your house."

"For what?"

"For dinner."

"You wouldn't want to see my house."

"Actually, I would, so let's make it your place. Don't worry, I'll do the cooking."

She opened the calendar on her computer screen and studied it. "Friday night." She wrote the date on a piece of paper and slid it across the desk. "Remember, if you will, Mister Barnes, that if I had not taken the bull by the horns, so to speak, we would have never done anything when we were dating."

T.J. felt the skin on his face going up in flames.

"I'm not just talking about that," Mary Beth continued, pointing for him to pick up the note. "I'm talking about everything, going back to the beginning. Do you remember who had to invite whom to the junior prom?"

T.J. was still dialing through ancient memories when his cellphone rang. "It's Duke Cumberland, head of the Maryland State Police. I've got to take it," he told Mary Beth, tapping the phone and holding it to his ear. "Hey, Duke. What's up?"

T.J.'s tone changed immediately. "Where?" he asked.

18

A trooper waved T.J. past the roadblock and pointed to the flashing lights on a State Highway Administration dump truck. "In the culvert," he yelled, "straight down the bank from the truck."

In his long career, T.J. Barnes had been called to scenes he would never forget, and he knew from the phone call that this one was going to be as bad as any of them. He made his way down the steep grass to where Duke Cumberland and three of his troopers kept vigil over a bright yellow tarp.

The superintendent of the Maryland State Police greeted T.J. solemnly. "She's not a pretty sight, but I'll take odds it's your missing girl."

"Who called you?"

"The Public Works crew found her while they were cutting the bank and clearing the culvert channel. Their supervisor notified us because Sawmill Road is a state highway." Duke was quiet for a minute, staring up at the highway. "Looks to me like someone dumped her from up there on the shoulder like she was a bag of trash." He knelt and pulled back the tarp. "But that's not what killed her."

T.J. stared at the massive bruise on the young woman's hideously contorted neck. He was long past the point of recoiling at sights that would make most men vomit, but he would never stop being amazed at what one human being was capable of doing to another. His practiced scan took in the dead girl's long, mud-soaked hair, her sightless blue eyes, and the pallid white skin of her bare body. He looked at it because it was his job to look. When he was finished, he replaced the tarp and spoke over his shoulder to Duke. "We took fingerprints from her car that will provide a positive ID, but there is no doubt in my mind that this is Patricia Dugan."

In death, in front of all these people, the young nurse's privacy had been violated to a point she could not have imagined when she was alive. T.J. was not going to give them anything else to gape at by pointing out that one of her legs was shorter than the other. The state medical examiner would make that clear enough in his report.

The ambulance crew was making its way down the bank with a stretcher. T.J. didn't know them all by name, but he knew their faces. He had seen them at traffic accidents, house fires, and countless other unexpected tragedies that cut life short. Today, they were not rescuers; someone sick and evil had made sure of that. They would shake their heads and do what they were trained to do, and then, as heartless as it had always seemed to T.J., morning would become afternoon and afternoon would turn into night as though nothing out of the ordinary had happened. As he climbed back up the steep bank, it came to him that one step in the awful business of dealing with tragic death would not be required of him this time. There was no door to knock on, no family members to bear unbearable news. Those experiences were as unforgettable as anything he had ever been through as a police officer.

19

Marie Anselmo blessed herself in a silent prayer of thanksgiving as she tasted the sauce. All three of her children would be together tonight. That was always a special occasion, but now, in a world that seemed to become more difficult to understand every day, seeing them at her table and knowing they were safe was a special gift from God. Rita's friend from the hospital had disappeared, a terrible mystery that made Marie want to hold her children in her arms the way she did when they were babies. She stirred a touch more wine into the sauce just as Vito's truck pulled into the long driveway outside the window. "You can heat the water for the pasta," she informed her mother, Nana Nuncio, who was grating cheese at the kitchen table.

Anthony Anselmo, who had picked up his brother, Dario, at the firehouse, parked behind his father. The two sons hugged Vito the way they had since they were little boys and followed him into the garage. Vito took a gallon jug of red wine from the tool shelf next to his workbench and reached for the coffee mug he kept on top of the garage refrigerator. Anthony helped himself to a less traditional Budweiser before collapsing onto the wide stairs leading to the kitchen and removing his mud-caked construction boots.

"I'm thinking one more week before we pour concrete at the hospital plaza job," Vito said, kicking off his own boots. "Jenkins Plumbing started running the pipes for the fountain today."

Anthony emptied his beer and nodded without saying a word.

"The electrician will be right behind them," Vito continued, slipping into the old pair of loafers he called his dinner shoes. "The concrete plant is waiting for us to give them the word. Eight truckloads. I double-checked the estimate today. Enough concrete to seal King Tut's tomb." He laughed his booming laugh and finished the wine before noticing that neither boy seemed to appreciate the joke. They were looking at him like they used to when something happened at school that they knew was not going to make him happy.

"Okay, you two, enough with that look. What is it?" he demanded, rinsing his cup in the laundry sink.

The brothers stared at each other. "Tell him, Dario," Anthony said.

"Tell me what?"

Dario closed his eyes, and as he had done countless times since he saw Patricia's lifeless body in a trash-strewn drainage ditch that morning, he prayed for her soul to rest in peace. "They found that missing nurse," he said finally. "Rita's friend from the hospital. I was on the ambulance crew that got the call."

"What do you mean, 'Got the call?' Is she hurt?"

"She's dead, Papa," Dario answered almost inaudibly.

Before Vito could react, Marie Anselmo opened the door at the top of the garage stairs. She issued three short announcements before retreating back into the kitchen. "Dinner is on the table. Leave your muddy boots in the garage. Bring the jug of wine."

Vito listened for the door to shut before he spoke. "Don't say anything about this to your mother or your grandparents. I will tell them after dinner."

"What about Rita?" Anthony asked. "She must have heard the news at the hospital."

Vito had not thought about that. He used an Italian expression forbidden to the boys when they were growing up and sealed the thought by blessing himself.

The big house was alive with aromas that every member of the family recognized from their earliest memories. The sauce, sweetened with red wine, had simmered all day, coaxing flavors from Nana Nuncio's meatballs, slices of eye-of-the-round, and spicy homemade sausage. The buttery pasta, sometimes spaghetti, sometimes rotini, filled hand-painted serving bowls that had belonged to Vito's mother, Nonna Giovanna, since she was a young bride. Family tradition dictated that salads were for Italian restaurants, not Italian homes. Rita and her two brothers never saw salad on a dinner table until they were old enough to eat at their friends' homes. The dinner green in the Anselmo house was steamed broccoli or Swiss chard, cooked in olive oil with capers and garlic, a Nonna Giovanna recipe so sacred that only she was allowed to make it.

Dario was still in his blue fire department uniform, a sight that always made his grandparents proud. He kissed them all and took his place at the table. After what had been the worst day of his career, he did not have the heart to kid his mother and grandmothers about how beautiful they looked or tell his grandfather Vincenzo that he looked more like Rudolph Valentino every day.

"Where is Rita?" Nana Nuncio asked.

"She's in her room," Marie answered. "She kissed me when she came home and went straight upstairs." Marie shrugged as she unfolded her napkin. "I guess her friend hasn't come home yet."

Dario looked at his father, his eyes filling with tears.

"What is going on?" Grandfather Vincenzo asked in Italian.

Vito finished his wine and refilled his glass. He did not know whether to stand or remain seated, but it was his uneasy responsibility as the head of the family to explain to his parents and his mother-in-law that Rita's friend Patricia, the young nurse who had been missing, was dead. He groped for words that would not shock or upset them but found that he could not disguise the horrible truth. He started to stand, then sat back down. The only time he could remember seeing Patricia was when Rita's car battery went dead and he had to meet her at the hospital with jumper cables. She had been a pretty girl, not as beautiful as his Rita but pretty in what he thought of as an Irish way, and unlike the women in his own life, she seemed shy and quiet. Rita told him the sad story about Patricia losing her parents, and because he could not imagine a life without family, he had never forgotten it. Unwelcome tears formed in his eyes. Beginning in English and answering their shocked questions in Italian, he explained why Rita was in her room.

When he finished, the family held hands and prayed for Patricia Dugan's departed soul. An Our Father, a Hail Mary, and a Glory Be. While they did, Vito opened his eyes and looked at the people who were his entire life, the people he loved. It was not tender love. It was not affection, warm and soft. It was an instinct born into a heart as aggressive and ferocious as that of a lion. His eyes found his daughter Rita's empty chair, and tears that did not make him feel ashamed streaked his face. As his family prayed, he swore an oath promising what he would do to anyone who ever laid a finger on his lovely daughter. There would be no forgiveness. There would be no mercy. Justice would not be left to the Lord or to the law. His fists tightened in anger. There would be no justice for anyone capable of such an unthinkable deed. There would only be vengeance, and that vengeance would be his. "Amen," prayed his family. "Amen," repeated Vito with so much feeling that all eyes turned to him.

20

Only one person at the Hargrove Police Station was privy to the incantations and manipulations required to bring the department's ancient coffee maker to life.

"You here yet, Helen?" T.J. called through his open office door for the third time.

"Not yet, Chief, but I'll be here any minute," one of the men answered in a falsetto voice.

T.J. managed to bite his lip. It was a bad morning for stupid humor, and it was a bad morning to try to concentrate on a medical examiner's report without another jolt of caffeine. He polished off what was left of the diner coffee he had picked up on his way in and reread the cold, straightforward language ruling Patricia Dugan's death a homicide. His eyes skipped the photographs he had forced himself to study the first three times and moved to the paragraph concluding that her badly bruised neck had been fractured approximately ten hours before the public works crew found her body in the drainage ditch on Sawmill Road. He counted the hours backward and came up with the same answer: The young nurse had died at approximately eleven-thirty the night before the sun came up on her naked and battered body.

He tossed the empty Styrofoam cup toward the wastebasket in the corner and missed. "Eleven-thirty, eleven-thirty," he thought aloud, "roughly five hours after she was last seen, and during that time, she was taken to a location that was three and a half miles from the hospital and approximately four and a half miles from her apartment." *Not exactly brilliant thinking,* he lectured himself, retrieving his errant throw and dropping it into the basket, *but everything means something.* It was one of his favorite reminders, and in this case, what the simple arithmetic told him was that Patricia Dugan had almost certainly been killed within a few miles of where he stood, staring at the county map on the wall. He circled his desk and sat back down, thinking. If he was right about the *where,* the *who* might well be someone he or his people had crossed paths with recently. "Mark," he called through the open door. "Got a minute?"

Like a genie, Sergeant Mark Jenkins appeared. "I was right outside the door trying to beg some coffee out of that damn machine."

T.J. was much too focused to remind the young officer that unless his name was Helen, he had no chance of figuring out the coffee maker—or the copy machine, for that matter. "I want you to check out everyone who works for that carnival outfit," he ordered. "Backgrounds, police records, the whole nine yards."

"Already on it, Chief. Corporal Suit and I figured that bunch of weirdoes is worth a hard look."

"How about the blue pickup truck?" Three different callers had reported that they saw a blue pickup truck driving with its lights out the night before Patricia's body was found.

"Nothing yet. The state police are helping us with that one."

Phone calls like that began while the first stories of Patricia's death were still airing on television and radio news programs. Three people reported that a seedy-looking man had been sleeping in a car in the Walmart parking lot. Another caller said that her next-door neighbor had hated nurses since his wife died in a hospital twenty years ago. T.J. had trained his staff to listen carefully to every call, even the ones that seemed completely nutty, and record every detail of the conversations no matter how unimportant they seemed. The case log showed that there had already been twenty-nine calls, including a report that a creature that looked like the abominable snowman had been spotted in the woods near Sawmill Road. T.J.'s people might laugh about reports like that after an arrest had been made, but they knew better than to do it now.

"What about the guy passed out in his car?"

"Harry Bonekirk. He's sleeping it off in a cell."

Everyone in the department knew that Harry was a danger to no one except himself, but they also knew without being told that they were expected to account for every hour of the man's last five days.

"Thanks, Mark," T.J. said, ending their meeting with a casual salute. "I hope it goes without saying that there won't be any vacation days until we solve this thing."

"Everyone knows that, Chief. I didn't have to say a thing."

When T.J. was alone again, he took the crime scene photographs out of the drawer where he had stacked them face down. Like the ones in the medical examiner's report, he had seen worse but never any that upset him more than these. The fact that Mary Beth thought the world of Patricia Dugan made dealing with her violent death personal to the point of distraction. He concentrated on studying the pictures objectively, but the strange realization that if he had a daughter, she would be roughly Patricia Dugan's age, made him angrier than he ever wanted to be when he was wearing his uniform. Photographs of girls Patricia's age should show them smiling and laughing with a bunch of friends at the beach or looking as beautiful as a princess on their wedding day, not cold and lifeless in police prints cataloged with certified time and date stamps. He forced himself to shuffle through the pictures again, looking for something, anything. Years ago, crime scene photographs had been printed in black and white. Not these. Patricia's skin was as white as paper, and the ugly bruise on her neck and shoulder was deep purple and sickening. Her long hair was streaked with mud and strands of wet grass. What did not show was the terror and panic that had been erased from her beautiful face by the last beat of her heart.

T.J. stood and faced the windows overlooking the courthouse, remembering what Vito Anselmo had said he would do to anyone who harmed his daughter, Rita. Vito had not gone into detail, but it didn't take a genius to understand that he wasn't talking about sitting in a courtroom and watching quietly while a zealous defense attorney distracted the jury with extravagant details of his client's difficult childhood or other sob stories. T.J. believed in the law. It was his life, but he wondered how many times he would have to cross the street to the courthouse and play his part in the snail-like games staged by prosecutors and defenders in which he would be called upon to testify to the facts as he knew them and answer questions, often with a simple yes or no, in a process that increasingly seemed to regard victims as legal details and stress the rights of worthless scumbags whose only regret was that they had been caught. There would be a conviction in Patricia Dugan's case, he would do his damnedest to see to that, but after that, there would be an appeal and then another appeal, and as all those months and years passed, the animal who did this terrible thing would be alive and a beautiful young woman would be dead.

"Do you think that standing there and staring out the window is going to find the killer of that young girl, Chief Barnes?"

T.J. turned, torn from his thoughts. Three members of the county council stood on the far side of his desk. June Buggs-Vosbeck was doing the talking, Hastings Dew was looking at the floor, and Achilles Lasko seemed to be doing his best to look like he meant business, a mask that melted when T.J.'s eyes met his.

"What she means, Chief Barnes...," Councilman Dew began, still looking at the floor.

"Hush, Hastings," June Buggs-Vosbeck snapped. "I am the spokesperson for this committee. We all agreed to that." She cleared her throat. "Chief Barnes, as chairperson of the ad hoc committee formed to solve this horrible crime, we have several questions for you."

T.J. took a deep breath, reminding himself that nonsense like this went with the territory. "I'll be happy to tell you what I can about an active investigation," he answered, leaning against the windowsill.

"You will tell us what we ask you," she flared. "Has the FBI been notified?"

"They have not. There is no evidence indicating that a federal crime has been committed."

"Make a note of that, Achilles," she ordered. "Have the Maryland State Police been notified?" was her next question.

"There was no reason to notify them. Colonel Cumberland and his men were first on the scene. We are working very closely with them, as always."

"Colonel Cumberland and his *men*?" June Buggs-Vosbeck bristled. "Colonel Cumberland and his *men*?"

T.J. was in no mood to play with pronouns. "They were, in fact, all men," he informed her.

"Chief Barnes, you are truly a dinosaur."

T.J. could not stop himself from delivering a line that would follow him for the rest of his life. "No. I am a Terrapin."

"I beg your pardon?" June Buggs-Vosbeck demanded.

Behind her, Hastings Dew, who had spent the better part of two years at the University of Maryland, smiled. "In college, he was a Terrapin, not a dinosaur. It's a joke."

June Buggs-Vosbeck exploded. "I will not tolerate such insolence. The first recommendation of this committee will be that you be fired as police chief. Make a note of that, Achilles." She spun on her heels and led her two-member committee toward the door where they ran into Helen Burgess who seemed overjoyed to see them.

"Are you here about the window replacements?" she asked excitedly.

"I know nothing about windows, Madam," June Buggs-Vosbeck replied indignantly. "I am the chairperson of an ad hoc committee."

"Ad hoc in your sock," Helen muttered as the chairperson and her committee squeezed past her.

There were times when T.J. wished Helen would keep her lip buttoned, but this was not one of them.

"Mary Beth," T.J. started when she answered the phone.

"I need to see you tonight," she interrupted.

There was a pause before T.J. answered that he was not going to be much fun by the time he got finished at the station.

"I don't need fun, T.J. I just need to be with you."

There was another silence while Helen slipped a rough copy of T.J.'s crime report onto his desk and tapped her finger on a half-dozen red-marked typos. He mouthed, "Fix them for me?" then a "Thank you."

"T.J.?" Mary Beth inquired into the phone.

"I'm still here. The press conference is next. I'm going to be dead tired by the time I get done."

"You will also be hungry."

Mary Beth's observation jolted T.J.'s memory. "I left some ground beef to thaw on my kitchen counter. I was planning to grill a couple of burgers before the day got so crazy."

"I'll take care of it. Do you have a key hidden somewhere at your place or is that a stupid thing for a police officer to do?"

T.J. almost managed a laugh. "It may be stupid, but I do it. It's under the clay flowerpot on my back porch."

"You have flowers?"

"Not really, but I do have flowerpots, three of them. The key is under the big one in the middle."

"Do you have any hamburger rolls?" Mary Beth asked, relieved to have something other than Patricia to think about.

"I don't know about rolls, but I'm pretty sure there is some bread left."

"I'll stop at the supermarket on my way over."

"Do you know where I live?"

"Of course, I know where you live. I drive by your house every once in a while to keep an eye on you."

T.J. expected her to laugh, but she didn't.

21

Waiting at a traffic light, Mary Beth closed her eyes and tried to understand what it is about human beings that allows them to live their lives knowing there is something important they really should do before all the tomorrows become yesterdays, and one day wake up to the fact that the chance to do what they always meant to do is gone forever. Time and again, she had intended to invite Patricia out to dinner or just kick back with her in the hospital cafeteria after work to make sure she understood there was someone she could talk to, day or night. It would have been unrealistic for anyone to think they could replace the motherly love and understanding that had been stolen from Patricia Dugan's life at such an early age, but maybe taking the time to reach out would have made living her short life a little easier.

The light turned green and red again, and still, Mary Beth didn't move. She had always meant to assure Patricia that her handicap was more than overshadowed by her goodness and beauty and that a good man, a truly good man, would feel that way and love her, regardless. A truly good man. The words made her think again of the yesterdays that were gone and the tomorrows that were never guaranteed. T.J. Barnes had once been her rock, and she needed him to be her rock again.

"Get your ass in gear, Lady!" the driver of a big-tired tow truck screamed as he leaned on his horn and swerved around her.

Mary Beth waved a wave of apology that the angry man answered with one finger.

The key was under the middle flowerpot just as T.J. told her it would be. Much more surprising to Mary Beth was the presence of marigolds in the two smaller pots and a geranium in the big one. They were desperately in need of watering, a situation she remedied with a half-filled watering can she found next to his kitchen door.

Inside, she set the grocery bag on the table and experienced another surprise; except for a coffee mug in the sink and a forest of yellow sticky notes on the refrigerator, the kitchen was as neat as her own. Convincing herself that if notes were meant to be private, they would not be displayed on a refrigerator door, Mary Beth put on her reading glasses. *WATER FLOWERS* assured her that T.J. did not intentionally abuse plants, and *CUT GRASS* meant he was aware that the grass in his yard was high enough to hide small animals. The most intriguing note read *DINNER*, but it was going to be tricky to ask him about that one without revealing that she had read them all.

Putting away the package of ground beef she found defrosting on the kitchen counter gave her a legitimate excuse for opening the refrigerator. Four cans of Miller Lite, a half-empty container of lactose-free milk, a pint of strawberries, and a bottle of ketchup were arranged neatly on the clean glass shelves. Other than the Miller Lite and possibly the ketchup, it could have been the refrigerator of a monk. To these sparse provisions, Mary Beth added the bottle of Pinot Grigio she had picked up at the grocery store. A second later, she took it back out, found a very clean glass behind the second cabinet door she opened, and filled it. Many times, maybe even most times, drinking was not the answer, but there were other times, good and bad, when it was indeed the answer. For the first time since Wade died, she found herself waiting for a man to come home to dinner. She sat at the table and sipped the cold wine, comparing the neatness of the two men. One of Wade's favorite sayings had always been *A place for everything and everything in its place*, and it appeared that T.J. lived by the same rule. She felt guilty about reading the refrigerator notes but not guilty enough to keep her from finding out if the rest of the house was as neat as the kitchen.

The living room and the small dining room were as uncluttered as a monastery, mainly because they were virtually unfurnished. A table lamp, its electrical cord plugged into a wall socket, sat on the dining room floor. There was no dining room table, no chairs, and no pictures on the wall. The living room seemed over-furnished by comparison. The room's décor—a term that caused her to smile—included a rack of aluminum TV trays, a sight Mary Beth had not seen since she was a teenager, but no television, a coffee table with an orderly stack of Maryland Terrapin coasters, and a rolled-up rug pushed against one wall. A cork dartboard with six darts—three crowding the bullseye—hung on the wall above an empty fireplace. A weightlifting bench in the middle of the room supported a fully loaded barbell. The workout equipment did not surprise her, but a purple African violet on the windowsill did. She took one step up the stairs before asking herself if she would want T.J. to do the same thing in her house. No such pang of conscience kept her from finding out what was behind the closed door at the bottom of the stairway. Opening it was like discovering an ancient tomb.

The last light of the day slanted through Venetian blinds, exposing a man cave as cluttered as the rest of the house was bare. Against the far wall, almost untouched by the intruding light, a tossed blanket and scattered newspapers half-hid a battered couch. The dying rays focused soft attention on a wide wooden desk and the wall it faced. Mary Beth tiptoed into the quiet space, sensing that she was an intruder in a sanctuary. The wall above the desk was covered with certificates of appreciation from everyone from the Boy Scouts to the Rotary Club, a display she had no way of knowing was kept up to date by T.J.'s sister, Beverly, who ignored his strenuous insistence that he would take care of arranging everything when he had the time.

The shelves of an old maple hutch were filled with dusty football trophies and framed photographs of teams he had played for at Hargrove High School and the University of Maryland. There was a single framed photograph on the desk that took her breath away. Mary Beth dropped into the worn swivel chair and held it in her hands. Locked in a dreamlike past, the two of them sat on the front steps of her sorority house. She could tell by the coat she was wearing and the candy cane pin on her collar that the picture had been taken right before the Christmas break—*the magical Christmas break*—when she was sure T.J. was going to ask her to be his wife. She had never in her life been so filled with joy and excitement as she was on the afternoon they posed for that picture, and only days later, she had never been so devastated. T.J. loved her then, she knew he did, just as she knew he loved her now. He wasn't the type of man to say it; maybe she would never hear him put it in words, but she knew he loved her. She returned the picture to its place on the desk, closed her tearing eyes, and wondered what T.J. thought about when he held it in his own hands.

22

When he got home, T.J. found Mary Beth asleep in his night-filled den. "I got away as soon as I could," he apologized, shaking her gently before switching on the desk lamp. "I picked up a pizza at Luigi's. It's too late to cook."

Mary Beth had been dreaming about the worst Christmas Eve of her life. In front of the Christmas tree, with her parents already in bed, a shaken T.J. told her about responding to a robbery scene in which bullets grazed the hood of his police car and sent shards of steel into his arm. He took off his jacket and showed her a blood-spotted bandage that stretched from his wrist to his elbow. Looking somewhere over her shoulder rather than into her eyes, he told her that it would be wrong for him to marry her when any day spent in uniform might be the day he left her a widow and their children fatherless.

In real life, she had been too young and wounded to say anything except, "Please don't do this, T.J.," but in the dream, she was her grown self. "An accountant can be run over by a car. A construction worker can be killed on the job," she had the dream-wisdom to argue. "Anybody can die, T.J., but people can't refuse to live because they are afraid of dying."

She stared at the picture on the desk, then up at T.J. "You lived all these years. You came home every day," Mary Beth told him, too confused by sleep to realize that she had said it aloud.

T.J. followed her eyes to the faded Christmas picture. He wanted to tell her that he thought the same thing every time he sat at his desk and looked into the past, but the only words that came to him were "How could I know?"

They sat at the kitchen table eating pizza and drinking coffee. T.J. did not know what to do with his eyes, and Mary Beth could not stop thinking about the night when for her, Christmas memories became forever confused with shattered dreams. To fill the quiet, T.J. said he remembered that she used to like pizza with pepperoni and black olives.

She smiled, pulling her chair closer to the table. "I still do."

"Luigi's kids run the place now. Only they aren't kids anymore."

She shook her head. "His son Mario was a freshman when I was a senior at Hargrove High School."

Any other time, small talk like this would have bounced from one memory to another, triggering smiles and laughter. On this night, a heavy presence in the room overpowered their attempt to avoid the inevitable.

"Do you know yet what happened to Patricia?" Mary Beth finally managed.

T.J. stood, walked over to the kitchen counter, and refilled his cup. "We received a preliminary report from the state medical examiner this afternoon. Without going into unpleasant details, I can tell you that whoever did it is a very strong individual."

"Meaning she was killed by a man?" she answered, taking time to let the painful images settle.

"That's a safe assumption."

The worst of Mary Beth's fears fought to be heard. "Was she raped?"

T.J. shook his head. "No."

His answer surprised and confused her. "Then why? What possible reason could anyone have for killing a sweet person like Patricia?" She finished her coffee slowly. "It's hard to imagine that she had an enemy in the world."

T.J. shook his head as he refilled her cup. "We have a lot of work to do, but we will find and arrest the person who did it."

"And then what? The monster who did it will be paroled after twenty years, and poor Patricia will still be dead." She closed the pizza box, reached for his plate, and stood up. "I say bring back hanging."

T.J. looked at her, trying to decide if she was serious.

"I mean it, T.J. Whoever did this does not deserve to live."

"We can't live outside the law, Mary Beth," he said quietly. "If we do, the whole thing falls apart, and we are no better than the animal who did this."

They looked at each other, sharing the thought that it would be best to change the subject. Mary Beth did that with a confession. "I read your refrigerator notes, and I think I know what the one that says *Dinner* means."

T.J. turned the same shade of red she remembered him turning when she asked him a million years ago if he was ever going to kiss her.

"My answer is yes," she informed him without mercy.

23

Olga's people had very little in common with members of the human race who lived in houses without wheels, cut grass on Saturdays, went to church on Sundays, and had no particular reason to wish they were somewhere else when approached by a police officer. Virtually every ride jock and ticket-taker on her payroll had something to hide and associated sharply pressed shirts and polished brass with the kind of trouble they thought they had left behind when they jumped aboard a traveling carnival.

On the first day of what T.J.'s officers explained were routine background checks, Olga lost Rubin Roach, her Tilt-A-Whirl operator, on an outstanding non-support warrant and was forced to replace him with a peanut hawker whose unfamiliarity with the ride's braking system touched off several never-to-be-forgotten experiences. On the positive side, with cops swarming all over the lot, Olga noticed a drastic reduction in the marijuana fumes escaping from her sleeping busses and a major drop in hip-pocket bottle sightings.

"Are you kidding?" Olga replied when she was asked to account for her time since the carnival rolled into town. "If I'm not fixing a broken ride or roaming around the lot keeping a sharp eye on things, I'm back there in my trailer, catching a few hours' sleep or working on the books." She cocked a thumb over her shoulder, indicating a small yellow and orange RV at the rear of the lot.

"Mind if we take a look?"

"Knock yourself out; it isn't locked."

The two young policemen were hurrying toward the trailer when Olga called after them, "I hope I didn't leave my silk nighty on the floor."

They stopped dead, no doubt staggered by the image of a woman with blacksmith arms wearing lingerie.

Olga's satisfaction with the word bomb she had hurled at them was cut short by the sight of Dixie Carter, the funnel cake cashier, slipping money into her oversized bra. As much as she wanted to wring the woman's fat neck on the spot, she wasn't about to risk trouble with the police on the very night when the life of a certain unsuspecting nurse was going to change forever.

"Step right up and purchase the winning ticket on this beautiful Harley Road King!" Jerry Donnelly shouted into a microphone as he spun a barrel-sized basket half-filled with ticket stubs. "Five dollars a book, six books for twenty-five dollars! Just feast your eyes on this black and gold beauty! Check out those leather saddlebags! Get a load of those cool chrome mirrors! Step right up, Folks! Step right up!" he bellowed at the would-be bikers crowding the stage.

The big Harley was a beauty, Olga wouldn't argue with that. If she were a biker, a few books of chances might have been a temptation, but she wasn't a biker. She was a Cadillac person, and before this night was over, she reminded herself with a secret smile, her strong hands would find themselves holding the winning ticket on a brand-new Eldorado, silver with leather seats and all the options Lester's money could buy. The thought of slipping behind the wheel of a car like that tingled the hair on her brawny arms, a sensation that reminded her of the days when she climbed the short stairs of a thousand wrestling rings and slipped through the ropes. The plan was set. She knew to the minute what time her little Italian beauty left the hospital, and with her eyes closed, she could find the house on Olive Street where the cannolis, whatever the hell they were, would be waiting like bait on the back porch. She wanted the clock to race. She could not wait for a life without motorcycle raffles, broken rides, and employees like Dixie stealing her blind.

Lost in thoughts of living like a queen, Olga did not notice the coiling clouds twisting into position above the carnival grounds until the crack of thunder split the sky. Jerry Donnelly flinched but carried on, announcing that for one hour—and one hour only—raffle tickets could be had for half price, an announcement that prompted many in the crowd to wave dollar bills at him. Seconds later, his microphone shorted out in a drumming downpour.

"You know the drill, People!" Olga screamed like the captain of a floundering ship as the carnival crew, intimidated by her fury, ignored the rain and went to work. Tent flaps were buttoned up while seats were unhooked from the Ferris wheel and stacked upside down on the puddling ground. Tarps were flung over cotton candy kiosks and popcorn machines and tied down with the practiced precision of sailors in a storm before anyone dared to flee for the cluttered RVs and rusty busses to break out the booze and cards.

Olga changed her mind about delayed justice and grabbed Dixie as she dashed for the busses with her apron over her head. "Twenty dollars by this time tomorrow. Understand?"

"Twenty dollars!" the startled woman exclaimed, twisting futilely against Olga's vice-like grip. "All I took was one five and a couple of ones!"

"Twenty dollars or I kick your ass," Olga repeated ominously before flinging the woman back into the stream of fleeing workers.

After a hurried inspection of every tent and ride on the lot, Olga retreated to her trailer at the edge of the woods. Her shoes were full of water; she was soaked to the skin, but the usual rain rage was missing. What difference did a washed-out night mean, she crowed, when she was one final takedown away from raking in more money than she had ever seen in her life?

Olga stripped down and put on dry clothes. She was almost giddy, an unfamiliar feeling quickly stamped out by the determination to win that fueled her. She lay down on her cot and closed her eyes the way she always did before a big match. Into a mental photograph of mocking high school cheerleaders, she inserted Rita's lovely face. It was showtime.

24

Out on Olive Street, things were not going well.

Josephine Capparelli had no ricotta cheese, and without ricotta cheese, there could be no cannolis. No real cannolis. That truth had been as sacred to her mother as it had been to her grandmother, and Josephine was not about to question tradition like that. She refused to use mascarpone cheese like some Italian bakers did, and she would rather dye her hair red and dance a jig before she filled cannolis with cream cheese.

"I'll run up to the supermarket," her husband Sam offered, opening his newspaper. "They got a million kinds of cheeses in the back near the milk."

Josephine glared at a man who, after forty years of being married to her, should have known better. Supermarket ricotta was not in the same league with the ricotta her supplier, Mr. De Angelo, got from his brother in Palermo, and as any stunado knew, Palermo was where cannolis were invented.

Mr. Capparelli shrugged. "So, what's the problem? Did DeAngelo's truck break down again?"

Josephine walked to the kitchen door and looked out into the rain. Without turning around, she said, "If you must know, his brother Pepe got married and went to Greece on his honeymoon."

Sam looked up from the paper incredulously. "DeAngelo's brother got married! How old is he?"

"Eighty-one."

"You gotta be kidding," he laughed. "An eighty-one-year-old man on a honeymoon? What's he going to do for excitement on their wedding night? Pinch her butt?"

Turning quickly from the door, Josephine glanced nervously at the crucifix above her oven and blessed herself. "Such talk," she said. She was putting away the wooden cannoli shapers that had been her mother's and her grandmother's when she remembered something.

"Don't forget we're babysitting tonight at Ursula's house," she told Sam.

"It's on my schedule."

"What schedule? Since the bakery closed, you do nothing."

"Yeah, yeah," her husband mumbled, smoothing his newspaper against the table. "I see where they still haven't caught whoever killed that poor young nurse," he said, shaking his head. "We got a monster on the loose in this town."

Josephine looked out the door again. "For all I know, there's a monster hiding in that overgrown mess you call a backyard."

"Don't worry about it."

"What do you mean, don't worry about it? We could wake up dead in our beds."

Sam dismissed her concern with a wave of his hand. "We got a good police department. I like that guy Barnes." An article caught his eye as he turned the page. "Speaking of the police," he called out, tapping the newspaper, "says here that they haven't had any serious problems at the firemen's carnival this year. Mama Mia, do you remember the last one?"

Josephine wasn't listening. What Sam had said about that terrible business with the missing nurse made her remember that the nice Anselmo girl, who was supposed to come by tonight and pick up a box of cannolis, was also a nurse. "I got to make a phone call," she told her husband, hurrying from the kitchen.

"Rita, Honey, this is Mrs. Capparelli." She listened for a second. "I'm fine, thank you, but I have some bad news. I won't be making any more cannolis for a while, so there won't be a box on the back porch for you tonight."

Her free hand reached out for understanding as she listened. "I know your father loves them, God bless him, but Mr. DeAngelo's brother got married, and there goes the ricotta." Before Rita had time to ask, Mrs. Capparelli explained, "It's a long story. You tell your father happy birthday, and I will give him, what do you call them, a rain check."

She switched the phone from one hand to the other, smiling. "Thank you for being so sweet about it. And listen, Honey. You be very careful until they catch whoever did that terrible thing to the other nurse. You hear me?"

"Okay. God Bless," she added, deciding she might as well let Sam buy some supermarket ricotta and experiment with it. It was true that Mr. DeAngelo's brother Pepe was very old, and who knew, if he wasn't careful, he might die from a heart attack pinching his bride's butt or whatever. There was no harm in trying. If the cannolis weren't any good, she could always throw them in the garbage.

25

"Everything okay?" Mary Beth asked as Rita hung up the phone.

A smile wiped the disappointment from the young nurse's face. "I'm afraid you almost heard me swear in Italian. That was Mrs. Capparelli. She can't make cannolis for my father's birthday this year."

"Mrs. Capparelli? Have they reopened?"

Rita shook her head. "They're still trying to get the roof of the bakery fixed, but in the meantime, Mrs. Capparelli is taking orders at her house."

"So why no cannolis?" Mary Beth asked, turning off her computer for the day.

Rita stopped at the door. "It seems that she can't get the right kind of cheese because somebody got married."

Mary Beth stood up and stretched. "I don't follow."

"Don't try. Only in Italy."

Mary Beth laughed, shooing Rita away from her office and turning out the lights.

As Rita headed back to the nurses' station to get her things, Mary Beth called after her. "You go home and give your father a big birthday kiss. He'll like that better than a hundred cannolis." The elevator chimed like the period at the end of her sentence.

Downstairs, a young policeman came out of the hospital chapel just as Rita was going in. "Evening," he said, holding the door open for her. "I was just…" he hesitated uncertainly when their eyes met. "I mean, the hospital is part of my regular beat ever since that poor…" Once more, he hesitated, belatedly aware of the nurse's nametag visible inside Rita's unzipped jacket.

"You mean ever since Patricia Dugan died," Rita said quietly. "I was just going in to say a prayer for her before I go home."

"Cool jacket," he tried, hoping to keep her from disappearing so quickly. "I'm a big Orioles fan myself." Before he had a chance to ask, Rita explained that the name *Slugger*, embroidered below the Oriole Bird, was what her father called her when she played softball in high school.

"Cool."

Even after a long day at the hospital, Rita Anselmo was as beautiful a woman as Nick Suit had ever seen. He wanted the conversation to continue, but the only words that flashed through his mind were embarrassingly dumb. "I'm Officer Suit," worked until it dawned on him that he was now a corporal.

"Nice to meet you, Officer. I'm Rita Anselmo." She had always been told not to shake hands with a man unless he extended his hand first. Tomorrow, she would ask Mary Beth if that was still the rule, but since Officer Suit was too busy staring at her to notice the hesitation, the moment passed. "I better get going," she told him, nodding toward the chapel.

"Of course, of course," he answered before it dawned on him that his hospital assignment gave him a legitimate reason to ask if she had a safe way of getting home. "I mean, it's dark outside, and after what happened and all," he added so she wouldn't think he was trying to pick her up.

"My car is in the parking lot," Rita informed him, pushing open the chapel doors.

Rita blessed herself and searched for the right words. *May Patricia's soul rest in peace* and *May perpetual light shine upon her*, memorized pleas she repeated every night for her grandfather, Nanu Antonio, seemed much too automatic. Before Patricia died, Rita had never paid attention to the words. *Perpetual*, she realized, meant forever, meaning that like her grandfather, Patricia was never coming back. No more Patricia Dugan smiles. No more making a fresh pot of coffee for the people on the next shift before she went home, no more angelic kindnesses to patients. If there was a Heaven, Rita knew in her heart that Patricia was already there. She immediately begged God to forgive her for using the word *if*. There *was* a heaven. If there wasn't, nothing about what had happened made sense. No matter how horrible Patricia's death had been, she was at peace now with God's arms wrapped around her. Rita buried her face in her hands, trying not to think about what Patricia's final hours were like. Her shoulders shook as she sobbed uncontrollably. She had come to the chapel to pray, but the words now hardening her heart were godless curses on whoever did such a terrible thing.

A woman touched Rita's shoulder and whispered that Saint Joseph's was an excellent hospital and that whoever she was praying for was getting the best care possible. "God is good," the woman assured her. With restraint she found almost impossible to summon, Rita nodded her thanks, blessed herself, and left.

Outside, orange lanterns dotted the perimeter of the plaza construction area. Beyond them, a police cruiser idled with its headlights tunneling into the rain. "Need me to drive you to your car?" Nick Suit called to Rita as he reached across the front seat of the cruiser and rolled down the window.

"I'm good, thank you," Rita answered, hurrying into the rain-swept parking lot.

The young officer watched her until the distant car she entered came alive with light. He wanted to follow her home, not to learn where she lived, he tried to convince himself, but to make sure she got there safely. He continued to wonder if he was doing the right thing until the red taillights of her car disappeared into the wet night. Reluctantly, he turned his eyes back to the hospital. Chief Barnes had instructed him to keep an eye on things at Saint Joseph's until the end of his shift, and that was what he was going to do. A few seconds later, the lights of a second vehicle lit up like eyes in the night and began following Rita Anselmo. Nick Suit didn't notice, and even if he had, there was no way he could have known what was happening. He would tell himself that until he was too old to remember.

Olga Muntz was insane with impatience by the time she spotted Rita Anselmo making her way through the forest of wet cars. "You're late, Sweetheart," she whispered in the dark, trying to read the unlit clock on the Bronco's dashboard. Her smoldering hatred of cheerleaders and pretty girls in general was quieted by the thought that this one would never keep anyone waiting again. "Beauty isn't forever, my dear," she laughed witchlike as she watched Rita unlock the door of her small car and duck out of the rain. Olga knew Lester Turner. She knew how unpredictable and spoiled he was, and she knew that someday, he would grow tired of this new plaything the way he had grown tired of everything else in his pampered life, and when he did, he would dump her like he had dumped the others into the unforgiving depths of the lake in front of his mansion. She took one last drag of her cigarillo, tossed it into the rain, and eased the Bronco into place behind a princess whose charmed life was about to become a living hell. The police car parked in front of the hospital didn't move. *So far so good,* Olga smiled to herself.

The headlights in Rita's rearview mirror went unnoticed as her thoughts returned to Patricia Dugan. Patricia was dead, and that was very difficult for her to understand. The only other person in her life who had died was her grandfather Antonio, but he was an old man like people are supposed to be when they die, not sweet and young and caring like Patricia. Her grief turned to anger when she remembered how, as a little girl, she watched her family kneel in prayer as Nanu Antonio left the world surrounded by people he loved, not in some unimaginable nightmare like… "Stop! Just stop," she repeated until she calmed down.

The rain streaked the VW's small windshield in annoying arcs, distracting Rita with a reminder to ask her father to replace the wiper blades. She leaned forward and tried to concentrate on her driving. Essex Street was next. In a few blocks, she would pass Holy Rosary Church where her parents were married and where she and her brothers had gone to grade school.

The church would be locked up at this hour or she would have stopped and tried once more to pray for Patricia. She wanted to try again, thinking only of Patricia and not the monster who had done such a horrible thing.

The sight of Holy Rosary's softly glowing stained glass reminded her that the grotto behind the church was always open. Rita tried to read her watch in the dark. The family would understand if she was a little late. Her father's birthday dinner was important, but finding a quiet place to pray for Patricia was something she had to do before she did anything else.

Following Rita's taillights, Olga's adrenaline level reached the pre-fight high she had always found so intoxicating. *What a sweet setup,* she kept telling herself, an empty house on a long, lonely street where no one would be home to see or hear a thing. Her muscles tightened in anticipation of slipping up behind the unsuspecting girl and locking her in the Strangle Hold that had made her famous. *Just enough pressure,* she reminded herself. *Damaging the goods could cost you a lot of money.* Olga's smugness became a question mark when Rita's car slowed suddenly and turned into the driveway of a steep-roofed structure with the tall, arched windows of a church. She was confused. This was not the way to Olive Street; she knew that from her test runs to check out the house where a box of nurse bait waited on the back porch.

Olga pulled over to the curb and turned off the Bronco's headlights. From the street she watched Rita follow the empty driveway to an unlit parking lot behind the church. She gunned the big engine impatiently, trying to figure out what was going on.

Vito Anselmo, a man more religious than he wanted anyone to know, had built and paid for the Holy Rosary grotto, a spiritual oasis where from early morning to late at night anyone, Catholic or not, was welcome to escape the busy world and take time to look inward. From the time she was a little girl, the grotto had been one of his daughter Rita's favorite places.

The investigation that would begin before this rainswept night was over noted that the church secretary had forgotten to call an electrician about the timer that was supposed to keep the parking lot lights burning until 10 p.m. Olga knew nothing about any of that. All she knew was that this new setup was going to work just fine. With the Bronco's headlights still off, she coasted silently down the driveway, straining to catch sight of her prey.

Under the cover of the beautiful gazebo she had watched her father construct, Rita knelt before a garden of reassuring candles, trying with all her might to empty her mind of anger and concentrate on praying for Patricia's soul. The sound of rushing footsteps distracted her just as words that felt right began to flow. She started to turn but Olga was on her like a pouncing tiger. Hard muscles tightened in the vise-like clamp perfected in a hundred wrestling rings. *Not too hard,* Olga reminded herself as Rita struggled frantically to breathe.

26

The Anselmo family joined hands around the table and bowed heads, saying grace in English but by family tradition, ending with the words *buon appetito* with enthusiasm that sounded like a cheer. The wonderful aroma of eggplant parmesan, Vito's favorite since childhood, filled the room as three generations of his family raised stemless glasses in a birthday salute. As always, when touched by those he loved, Vito Anselmo, a man as strong as a bear, was overwhelmed with feelings that filled his eyes with tears. The moment was perfect in every way except one. His beloved Rita's chair was empty.

"Something came up at the hospital. She's on her way," Marie Anselmo explained with a straight face, hoping to keep Rita's cannoli mission a secret. Vito thought no more about it until, as family chatter gave way to the enjoyment of wonderful food, he noticed his wife stealing looks at her watch.

"Everything okay, Marie?" he asked across the table.

Marie was torn between ruining Vito's birthday surprise and the uneasy feeling that Rita should have been home long before this. When she realized that everyone was looking at her, she stopped pretending. "Rita was going to pick up a box of cannolis at the Capparelli's house on her way home, but…" This time she made no secret of checking her watch.

"It's raining, Ma," her son Dario offered, snatching the last piece of Italian bread before Anthony did. "Traffic is probably a mess."

"Call the hospital, Dario," Vito interrupted. "Maybe something did come up."

A minute later, Dario returned to the table, shaking his head. "They said she left over an hour ago."

"Do you have the Capparellis' phone number?" Vito asked his wife, pushing away from the table.

"Sit down, Vito. It's your birthday. I'll call them."

"I'm sure she will be here any minute," Anthony assured the silent table as he raised his wine glass. "Happy birthday, Papa."

Nonno Anselmo repeated the wish but his heart was elsewhere. He bowed his head and moved his lips in prayer. Before Vito could assure his father that there was nothing to worry about, Marie came back into the dining room. "There was no answer at the Capparellis' house," she announced quietly.

The muscles in Vito's big chest tightened. "Maybe that piece of junk she drives broke down," he said as lightheartedly as he could manage. More than once,

Rita had turned down his offer to buy her a new car, insisting that she loved her beat-up Volkswagen. "Besides, it's cute," she kidded him with the beautiful smile that had the power to melt his heart. "Anthony," he directed, rising from the table, "you and Dario drive to the hospital and see if she's broken down in the parking lot. If you don't find her, check all the gas stations along the way. I'm going to the Capparellis' house."

"They live on Olive Street," his wife reminded him.

"I know where they live," Vito said, trying to sound unconcerned as he touched her shoulder. "I'll be back before you know it—with Rita *and* the cannolis."

Vito felt the cold beginnings of panic when he saw that there were no cars parked in front of the Capparellis' house. He rang the bell and forced himself to wait for half a minute before pounding on the door with his fists. Four windows faced the wide front porch of the old clapboard house. The blinds were closed in two of them. The room inside the other two windows was too dark for him to see anything except the lighted rectangle of a door to a distant room. He followed a narrow path to the backyard, brushing against the untrimmed arms of rain-soaked bushes, a reminder that the Sam Capparelli he knew from weekly poker games was much better at running a bakery than he was at taking care of a yard. The light he had seen from the front windows illuminated a large kitchen with a windowed door facing the back yard. Vito was used to the sight of crucifixes, but until he hurried up the porch steps and looked in, he had never seen one keeping watch over an oven. He rapped on the glass and begged the God on the cross to send someone to the door. It was the first of several prayers that would go unanswered that night.

As he drove out of the neighborhood, he called Anthony on his cell phone. "Any luck?" he asked.

"Nothing, but we're going to backtrack and take another look. How about you?"

"Not yet, but there is one more place I want to check."

Vito had just remembered something. Rita told him that she was going to light a candle for her friend Patricia every day for the rest of her life. There were candles burning night and day in the grotto behind Holy Rosary Church, and Rita drove right by the church on her way home from the hospital. Sudden hope eased his growing fear. Holy Rosary had been Rita's church since the day she was baptized. It was the Anselmo family church. He drove as fast as he dared on the wet roads. A red traffic light stopped him but not for long. He looked both ways and kept going, reaching again for his cell phone and calling his neighbor Mary Beth Banakowski to ask if she had T.J. Barnes' personal phone number.

27

Mary Beth gave T.J.'s phone number to Vito and asked if anything was wrong.

He hesitated, not wanting to alarm her.

"Vito?" she pressed gently.

"Rita hasn't come home from work."

Mary Beth checked the time. "She was getting ready to leave the hospital when I left, and that was two hours ago."

Somewhere along the line, in grade school or high school, Vito couldn't remember which, a teacher had managed to fuse religion with common sense by telling a classroom full of kids to pray like everything depended on God but to act like everything depended on them. He remembered those words now, as he had many times over the years, and prayed harder than he had ever prayed in his life that he would find Rita in the grotto and take her home to her family. To show God that he was doing his part, Vito dialed the phone number Mary Beth had given him. Vito liked T.J. Barnes. He always had. T.J. was a common-sense guy with an entire police force he could call on to look for Rita. Between God and T.J. and his two good sons, Vito liked the chances of bringing his little girl home.

Olga drove like a model citizen, slowing for yellow lights she normally ignored and laying off the horn when she encountered drivers she suspected were escapees from some home for idiots. "No traffic tickets tonight," she reminded herself, glancing again into the rearview mirror. "You are much too close to winning the biggest bout of your life to get knocked off your feet now."

She eased past Michele's florist shop, checked to make sure there were no other cars in sight, then cut off her headlights and turned into the old church's abandoned parking lot. Blinded by the starless night and what remained of the rain, Olga failed to see what was left of a deteriorating curb and hit it hard. "Everything okay back there?" she laughed when she heard a moan from the back of the Bronco.

A football field away, the lights of the railroad crossing flashed red, and seconds later, the nightly freight train roared toward Baltimore with the power of an earthquake. Rita moaned again and tried to open her eyes. "Almost there, Sweetie," Olga whispered as she lifted the limp body onto her wide shoulders and followed a dancing flashlight beam through the front door of the church and down the steep cellar stairs. Freeing one arm, she pulled the string of the bare light bulb and kicked at a screeching shadow as it disappeared under the remains of the dead boiler. "Home sweet home," Olga laughed, dumping Rita onto a cot still littered with Patricia's clothes. She opened a bottle of water and splashed her new prisoner awake. "Let's get you out of these clothes and see if you are the gem I think you are."

As Rita struggled to understand who was speaking to her, the image of a grinning face spun slowly into focus. "You?" she finally managed.

"Me!" Olga laughed, reaching for the zipper on Rita's orange and black baseball jacket. "Time to see what we have here." After what happened with the last one, Olga was going to check every inch of this one's body like an inspector in a meat factory.

One of Vito Anselmo's many gifts to Holy Rosary Parish had been the installation of a timer programmed to keep the parking lot and grotto lights behind the church burning until ten o'clock every night. As part of the gift, he set up a service contract with his regular electrical contractor to make sure the lights worked when they were supposed to work. When Vito pulled into the parking lot, the only signs of light came from the flickering clusters of votive candles in the grotto. He braked hard and aimed his headlights up the long grotto walk. There was no one there.

"Rita!" he shouted, running up the walk. He kicked something. A shoe. The kind of shoe Rita told him all the nurses wore at the hospital. Clogs, she called them. He picked it up and held it against his chest. "Rita!" he screamed again, begging for an answer.

"Vito!"

He spun around and saw a running figure silhouetted against the flashing red-and-blue strobes of a police car. "Any sign of her?" T.J. Barnes asked breathlessly.

"A shoe! One lousy shoe!" Vito answered before hurling it with all his might toward the stained-glass windows overlooking the grotto. Cursing, he searched the ground for something else to throw. "Every Sunday, I come to this church and pray for just one thing! I pray for my family to be healthy and be safe, and look what happens!" He raised his eyes to the dark dome of the trees above the grotto. "Why did you do this to me, God? Why did you take my Little Rita?"

T.J. searched for words to calm him. Reassurances like *Everything is going to be okay* rang hollow when there was no way of knowing if that would be the case. What T.J. said, and what he hoped Vito believed, was that he and his people, Duke Cumberland and his state troopers and anyone else they needed, would do everything possible to find his daughter. He started by asking Vito if the Volkswagen in the parking lot belonged to Rita.

Vito did not seem to hear him. His eyes narrowed. He grabbed T.J. by both arms and pulled him close. "I'm going to kill whoever did this," he said quietly. "I'm going to find them and tear them apart with my bare hands."

It had been T.J.'s experience that promises of revenge, no matter how viciously spoken, were natural outlets for anger and frustration. He had heard hundreds of them, but this one, coming from a man like Vito Anselmo, had the ring of a solemn vow. He skipped the *Let The Law Handle This* lecture and concentrated on locating the spot in the dark bushes where the shoe had landed. Like examining every inch of the Volkswagen in the parking lot, finding that shoe was part of a police investigation that would not end until Rita Anselmo was found and returned to her family. The other possibility at the end of that process was one that T.J. refused to consider.

28

"I'm afraid to ask how your day went," Mary Beth said as T.J. hung his hat and gun in the closet next to the cellar door.

He collapsed into a kitchen chair, glanced at the refrigerator, and started to get up again.

"I'll get you one," Mary Beth said, signaling for him to stay put.

He leaned back and stared at the ceiling. "What a day," he exhaled.

"Did Vito Anselmo call you again?" she asked, setting the cold beer in front of him.

"Three times. The man is like a bear with a lost cub." T.J. took a long swallow. "He also showed up at my office while I was in a meeting with Duke Cumberland and two agents from the FBI."

"The FBI?"

T.J. nodded. "We don't have evidence of anything that fits their definition of a federal crime, but the Bureau has offered to help us in any way they can.

"And Vito? What did he do at the meeting?"

T.J. chose his next words carefully. "He mainly listened but it was obvious that he was ready to jump out of his skin." T.J. started to say something else but finished the beer instead.

"Say it," Mary Beth encouraged him.

"I was thinking about what Duke Cumberland said when Vito got up and left the meeting without saying a word."

"Which was?"

"If we don't get our hands on whoever did this before that man does, somebody is going to be picking up body parts."

The timer on the stove intruded like an alarm clock. "Would that make you unhappy?" Mary Beth asked as she opened the oven door and released the welcome promise of a home-cooked dinner.

"You can't run a world that way, Mary Beth."

"What way?"

"Outside the law."

T.J. tilted the last drops out of the bottle, deciding that Mary Beth didn't want him to get started on that subject any more than he wanted to sound like a broken record. The sight of roast chicken, mashed potatoes, peas, and steaming gravy delivered him to a place where he needed to be. Saying *thank you* to Mary Beth didn't seem like enough. He felt like kissing her.

"What?" she asked, catching him thinking about it.

"Please pass the potatoes." It was the best he could do.

Vito had gone to the police station that afternoon because he didn't know what else to do. He was on the verge of going crazy. He listened while T.J. Barnes informed the guy in the state police uniform and the two FBI agents that he had made arrangements with the board of education to borrow a school bus so his officers could drive the nursing staff home from the hospital, no matter where they lived. Vito had to stop himself from screaming that their damned school bus wasn't going to do his Rita or that poor Dugan girl any good now. He managed to keep the words to himself, but his fury must have escaped like the growl of an animal because they all stopped and looked at him before moving on. One of the FBI guys said they would send an agent to help the police interview everybody who worked at the hospital—*everybody*, the other one emphasized, from the CEO down to the guys who worked in the boiler room. When Vito told them he would like to listen to the interviews, someone said they didn't think that would be a good idea. He managed to hold his temper but lost it when one of the FBI agents referred to the *two* victims.

"Goddamn it, my daughter is alive!" he screamed, jumping to his feet.

The agent immediately apologized, explaining that there was no evidence that his daughter had been harmed. Vito had heard enough. He headed for the door.

"Not that way, Vito," T.J. Barnes called after him. "A bunch of people from the press are out there. Unless you want to talk to them," he added.

"I'm not talking to any damned reporters!"

T.J. called Helen into the office and asked her to show Vito the way to the back door. "The escape hatch," he called it. Vito liked T.J. Barnes. He always had, but right now, he was having trouble being friendly to anybody.

Outside, Vito didn't know what to do with himself. There was no point going to his office because all he would do when he got there was yell at people. He thought about checking out the hospital plaza project, but after climbing into his truck, he realized that all he wanted to do was find his daughter. He drove aimlessly, searching for he-didn't-know-what until he found himself circling through a small industrial park where he saw a sign for Thompson's Truck Repair, a business whose owner had been pushing without success for a chance to service Anselmo Construction's trucks and heavy equipment. Vito did not have a good feeling for the guy; it was nothing he could put his finger on, but it was enough to keep him from doing any business with him. Vito had been polite at first—as polite as he ever was with people he didn't like—but the guy kept showing up with his sales pitch. The last time he did, Vito asked him if he had trouble understanding English, and the guy got all hot and said he understood English better than any greasy Wop did. Vito pushed back from his desk and invited the guy to step outside. The fight lasted two punches, Vito's big right hand being both the first and the second.

He had forgotten all about the guy when T.J.'s people asked him if he could think of anyone who had a grudge against him or might have a reason to want to get even with him. "I know one son of a bitch who does," Vito swore aloud, slamming on the brakes and climbing out of his truck. "There is one son of a bitch who has a big reason."

Thompson's Truck Repair occupied three bays of a one-story concrete block building. A dirt-crusted dump truck filled the space inside one of the open overhead doors, and a partially dismantled front-end loader occupied a second bay. The third overhead door was shut tight. Vito stared at the steel chain and heavy-duty padlock securing it, his head swimming with unbearable thoughts. He kicked hard at a pair of legs protruding from under the dump truck.

"What the hell!" yelled a grease-stained mechanic as he pushed clear of the truck.

"Open that door!" Vito screamed as the man struggled to his feet.

"What?"

"Unlock that damned door!" Vito repeated, grabbing the man and pushing him toward the locked work bay.

Butch Thompson, who was reassembling a transmission at the rear of the shop, picked up a heavy wrench when he heard Vito's voice.

"Where's my daughter?" Vito yelled when the two men came face to face. "Unlock that damn door!"

"What the hell do you think you are doing, Anselmo?" the garage owner demanded, cocking the wrench. "Get your ass out of here before I part your Guinea hair right down the middle!"

"Easy, Butch, easy!" the mechanic shouted, forcing his way between the two angry men. "Mr. Anselmo," he said breathlessly, "there is nothing behind that door but boxes of parts and a 1935 Packard that Butch works on in his spare time."

"What's behind that door is none of his damned business!" Butch bellowed.

The mechanic turned to face his boss. "Come on, Butch, you read about this guy's daughter in the paper. You would be going nuts too if that was your kid."

Vito and Butch unlocked their eyes. The mechanic took the key from Butch's hand and unchained the door. An elegant touring car with a torn canvas roof and four flat whitewall tires sat amid a scattering of greasy auto parts like a forgotten queen.

29

"My dear Olga, I trust that you are calling me with good news," Lester Turner purred into the telephone.

"How does a beautiful Italian Princess sound to you?"

"A Princess, how lovely. Is she unspoiled?"

Olga carried the phone to her trailer window and watched the sun rise over the wet carnival grounds. Unlike the first nurse, the second one had fought like a wildcat to keep from being undressed, leaving Olga no choice but to get rough with her. "A few bruises," she exaggerated, "but they will clear up in no time."

"You misunderstand me, my dear. Allow me to put it biblically. Has the young woman known man?"

"How the hell would I know, Lester? She isn't wearing a wedding band, if that means anything." Olga pounded on the window to shoo away a flock of birds that was tearing apart an abandoned popcorn bag. "I promise you one thing, you have never seen a finer body."

A few seconds passed before Lester replied. "Virginity is not an essential requirement, but it would add a degree of novelty to my little gatherings. Be that as it may, when shall I come for her?",

"The sooner the better," Olga told him, trying not to sound as excited as she was about saying goodbye to money problems for the rest of her life.

"I will require detailed directions from the interstate to the ivory tower where you have sequestered this lovely princess," Lester continued.

"It's no ivory tower, Lester. It's an old church that you can barely see from the road," Olga informed him. "Call me when you get here, and I'll lead you to it."

"A church. My, my," Lester chuckled as he took notes. "I have not set foot in one of those since I was a child."

"Don't forget the cash. Like they say, 'No tickee, no laundry.'"

"It will be removed from my vault the moment I hang up," Lester answered, smiling at Olga's unusual attempt at humor. "I will call you from some nearby location the moment I arrive."

"Two hundred and fifty thousand dollars," she reminded him, rapping again at the popcorn-loving birds.

The deadbeats who worked the carnival were staggering out of the sleeping busses one and two at a time. "Dixie, get your ass over here and clean up this popcorn mess," Olga hollered, opening her trailer door, "Before I..."

The thought of the pile of money Lester was about to dump in her lap took the teeth out of Olga's anger. She left the details of her threat to Dixie's imagination and went back into the trailer where she changed her socks, put on a clean sweatshirt, and dropped to the floor to do fifty quick pushups. Good moods were so foreign to Olga that she did not realize she was in one. She grabbed the sill of the small window and did fifty deep knee bends, wondering if Cadillac Eldorados came in both two-door and four-door models. "Why don't I take a little ride to my local Cadillac dealer and find out," she continued aloud with a cheerfulness that made her feel weird. Olga found a pair of dry shoes and laced them up, confident that the Italian Princess in the church cellar was not going anywhere. She would take a quick swing through the carnival, check out the rides and game tents, kick whatever butts needed kicking, then go check out some Cadillacs. If she had not been afraid of scaring away half her crew, Olga would have taken a deep breath, beat her chest, and whooped like Tarzan. Her ticket to Easy Street was on the way.

Rita woke up with a confused memory of hearing the wail of a train that began faint and far off, grew in volume until it shook the walls around her, then slipped away. In the silence that followed, a small army of screeching shapes scurried across the shadowy floor. She pushed herself onto her elbows and watched the small red eyes stop and stare at her before vanishing like little ghosts. She was dizzy. The side of her face ached, and her neck and shoulder were stiff. Her head dropped back onto the cot. With her eyes closed, the flickering candles in the grotto behind Holy Rosary Church and the face of the strange woman from the diner spun together in pieces that were impossible to put together.

When she awoke again, Rita's searching eyes found the steep stairs in a dark corner that the woman with the inhumanly hard body had carried her down like she was no more than a ragdoll. "Take off those clothes, every last stitch!" she remembered the woman demanding after throwing her onto the cot. With sudden embarrassment, Rita realized that she was still naked and began to dig through the clothes on the filthy floor around her. There were two pairs of underpants, the white ones she had been wearing and a pair of light blue ones that were not hers. Next to a rusting boiler, she spotted her bra and the light green scrub pants she had worn to the hospital. Fighting the pain in her neck and shoulder, she began dressing. Worse than the physical pain was the humiliation of remembering how the woman had stared at her nakedness, rolled her over with hands too strong to resist, and demanded that she walk, with nothing on, over to the stairs and back again. "Lester and his friends are going to love you, Honey," she had declared smugly. "Now get back on that cot and stay there."

Lester and his friends. Rita was sure that was what the woman had said. It made no sense to her. She didn't know any Lesters, and other than seeing her at Sissy's diner, she knew nothing about the strange woman who had appeared out of nowhere and dragged her into this nightmare.

In the weak light of the solitary bulb, Rita spotted her Baltimore Orioles jacket draped over one of the pipes that protruded like spider legs from the boiler. She managed to find one of her clogs, and between the cot and the wall, she spotted her hospital smock and pulled it on. There were other clothes scattered around the rotting cot that were not hers: another pair of scrub pants and, in the shadows at the base of the boiler, white shoes and a second hospital smock. Her aching shoulder made it difficult to hold the other smock up to the light, but she finally managed to do it long enough to read *Patricia Dugan, RN* on the nametag. Seconds of confusion gave way to the horrible realization that Patricia's life had ended here in this foul hole. She dropped her head into her hands. Rita hated to cry, but she could not help herself. The worst part was imagining how terrified and alone Patricia must have been, knowing that there was no one turning the world upside down to save her the way she knew her own father was already doing.

Rita was sure that no matter where this terrible dungeon was, her father would find her. She dropped back on the cot, remembering the night she had been shaken awake by a little girl's nightmare and ran crying into her parents' bedroom. Her father held her in his strong arms while she told him about the terrible witch who had snuck into her room and carried her to a dark and scary forest far, far away. He hugged her tight and told her there was no witch in the world who could stop him from rescuing his Little Rita.

"Even if the witch is as wicked as the one that was so mean to Snow White?"

"No matter how mean she is. If a witch or a monster or anything else ever tries to hurt you, I will make them go away forever," Vito whispered, trying to not wake up her mother.

"Even if it's the witch from *The Wizard of Oz* with the green face?"

"Even her."

"Promise, Daddy?"

He kissed her on the forehead. "Promise. Now you run along to bed."

She was an adult now, in the middle of a real nightmare, but she knew her father would find her, and when he did, the strange woman who had dragged her into this dark prison would learn the hard way how much Vito Anselmo loved his children.

30

Vito Anselmo traveled the county roads night and day in search of his daughter. His sons begged him to let them ride along, but he insisted that the best thing they could do to keep their mother and grandparents from going crazy was to maintain some sense of normalcy by getting up in the morning and going to work the way they always had.

"I will call you the second I find any trace of her," he assured them.

Anthony, the older of the two, reluctantly agreed and went about the business of overseeing the Anselmo Construction Company's work, including the Saint Joseph's Hospital project where the underground spring had been successfully capped and preparations for pouring the plaza concrete were at a critical point.

For the younger son Dario, obeying his father meant reporting for duty at the fire department by day and selling Cadillacs for his uncle Phil Palermo at night. Except for one week a year, Dario rode as an EMT on an ambulance crew. That one week, like everyone else in the department, he pitched in to conduct the annual safety inspection of every business in the county.

The only problem that Michele Chambers, the owner of Michele's Florists, had with the unannounced safety checks was the way the fire department inspectors always showed up at the worst possible time. This year, when two of them waltzed through the front door in their impressive blue uniforms, she had a line of customers at the showroom counter, deliveries for Saint Joseph's Hospital and Gattuso's Funeral Home ready to be rolled out to the loading dock, and floral arrangements for three weddings awaiting her final blessing.

"Feel free to take a look around," Michele called to them as patiently as she could manage when they paused to look at the goldfish in a large stone fountain that was the main feature of her showroom. "I got that exit light fixed you wrote me up for last year. If you see any new problems…," she started before being interrupted by a ringing telephone.

"Are those Lionheads?" Dario asked, walking up to the counter.

Michele nodded as she hung up the phone and made a note. "You know your fish."

"He knows every animal on earth," his partner, Mike, informed her. "Including the name of every bug in the firehouse."

Michele found this to be a very interesting trait in a fireman but was much too busy to pursue the subject. "While you are doing your inspection," she informed them, raising her eyebrows to signal that she was delivering a message, "keep in mind that I donate a dozen gift certificates to the fire department's Fourth of July Auction every year. Ask Chief Donnelly if you don't believe me."

"We'll just look with one eye," Mike answered good-naturedly. "Come on, Zookeeper, let's get started."

The only violation they found was a rear exit door blocked by a stack of crates with *Fall Wreaths* printed on them in bold orange letters. Instead of writing it up, they moved the crates themselves. It was easy enough to do.

Out on the loading dock, there was nothing to see except for the steeple of an old church half-buried in the woods on the far side of an overgrown tobacco field.

"My father told me that old place has been abandoned since the pastor ran off with all the church's money," Dario said, moving his eyes from the church to the railroad crossing farther down the road.

"Happened when I was still in high school," Mike remembered. "I'm surprised the place hasn't fallen down."

"Is it on our inspection list?" Dario asked.

Mike flipped the pages on his clipboard until he found what he was looking for. "A note here says, 'unoccupied,' which means it doesn't require an inspection."

Dario's eyes drifted back to the top of the steeple. "Aren't the carnival grounds over there somewhere?" he asked.

"On the other side of the trees behind the church. If you look hard enough, you can see the top of the Ferris wheel."

The church in the woods would not allow Dario to take his eyes off it. "Want to check it out anyway?" he asked.

"What, the Ferris wheel?" Mike asked.

"No, the church."

Mike checked his watch. "Better stick to the list. We have fourteen more inspections to do today."

Even after his partner had gone back inside, Dario remained on the loading dock, staring across the field as a flight of birds, white against a gray sky, rose from the distant trees and curved skyward above the church until they were no longer individuals but a small, bright cloud that stood strangely still, a sight that, like the call of the church, he would never forget.

"You coming, Anselmo?"

Dario turned and followed Mike back inside. There was no way he could have known. He would tell himself that for the rest of his life.

31

To those sitting near him on Sundays, Phil Palermo appeared to be an unusually devout Catholic, praying so intently with his head in his hands that he seemed oblivious to the ritual of sitting, standing, and kneeling that was as much a part of the Mass as the Gloria or the Creed. In fact, what Phil Palermo, "Central Maryland's Cadillac King," was doing was taking advantage of the one quiet hour in his week to negotiate with God.

"Lord," a typical proposal might go, "if you jack up new vehicle sales by 25 percent, I will drop an extra fifty in the collection every Sunday from now until"—a pause to think—"the First Sunday of Advent." Or "Dear God, if the sale of my condo in Ocean City goes through in the next two weeks, I will put a new set of tires on Monsignor O'Grady's car. Wholesale. No labor charge." God had apparently noticed the condition of the good Monsignor's tires because the condo sold before the deadline, allowing Phil to put a down payment on the big house in Rehoboth Beach that his wife Ursula had badgered him into buying. Because of occasional wins like this, Phil Palermo had become a firm believer in the power of prayer, a belief that, with his beloved niece Rita missing, was the only thing that kept him from taking to drink.

"Almighty God," he prayed behind the closed door of his office at Palermo Cadillac, "please bring Rita back safe and sound to her family and to me, her loving uncle." He paused when he realized that he did not know what he could possibly offer God in return for such an incredible blessing. Because he was married, he could not promise to become a monk. For the same reason, he could not promise to sell his Cadillac dealership and give the money from the sale to The Little Sisters of The Poor. Ursula's name was on the showroom mortgage, and though she was very fond of Rita, she was also very fond of their membership at Terrapin Creek Country Club and the new house they were buying at the beach. Pressured by an uneasy feeling that God was waiting for his offer, Phil split the difference, explaining that because of the mortgage, he would have to keep the dealership but promising he would talk to Ursula about not spending a month in Saint Thomas next winter *and* donate the profit he would make on the next two Cadillac sales to The Little Sisters. "Please God, bring her back," he pleaded. "Rita's mother, my wonderful sister, is out of her mind with worry, and my brother-in-law Vito is mad enough to kill someone." Phil had just made the sign of the cross and kissed his knuckles when his nephew Dario tapped on the office door.

"Reporting for duty, Uncle Phil."

"Dario! I thought you might take a few days off to help your father look for your sister."

Dario shook his head. "I would be riding around with him right now if he would let me, but since he won't, I'd much rather be working here than sitting at home worrying."

Phil nodded that he completely understood. "Anything new?" he asked.

Dario shook his head again. "The police are searching for her. My father is wearing out the tires on his truck looking for her, and the rest of us are going crazy. That and praying. By the way," he added to change the subject, "that's a great-looking Eldorado out there in the showroom."

"Just came off the truck today."

"Mind if I sell it tonight?" Dario joked.

"Be my guest," his uncle answered, laughing for the first time in days as his secretary pushed through the door and hurried over to his desk with a neatly wrapped package.

"These were just delivered," she informed him before turning uncertainly to face Dario. "I was so sorry to hear about your sister." That was as far as she got before becoming lost in emotion and making a quick exit.

"You'll have to excuse Cheryl. She means well," his uncle said, watching the door close.

"It's the same at the fire department. No one knows what to say."

"Maybe these will help," his uncle said as he started unwrapping the package on his desk. "In the meantime, get out there and sell some cars. It might help take your mind off... things." He could not bring himself to say Rita's name again.

Out in the showroom, someone was sitting in the spotlighted Eldorado. "Your customer, Dario," said the sales manager. "Go get her."

For the second time on a day he would never forget, Dario Anselmo was about to experience feelings he could not explain, feelings that hit him the second he leaned into the side window of the Eldorado and greeted a woman with a pair of shoulders that put his to shame. "She's a beauty, isn't she?" he managed to ask with what his uncle Phil had assured him was a natural salesman's smile.

"Cut the crap. How much?" the woman answered, gripping the steering wheel with hands as intimidating as her shoulders.

It was a question that customers usually danced around, running their fingers up and down the window sticker, kicking a tire or two, and asking to look under the hood at a tangle of wires and shapes they knew absolutely nothing about. A more experienced salesman might have handled the situation differently, but Dario wanted to show his uncle what he could do on his own. He checked the sticker and repeated the bottom number.

"I'll take it," the woman with the linebacker body said, sliding out of the car.

"You'll take it?"

"That's what I said, Junior."

Dario was in uncharted waters again. He had never heard of anyone strolling into the showroom and buying a Cadillac the way people bought a pair of shoes. "Our finance manager has someone with him right now, but I'm sure they won't be long," he said uncertainly.

"I don't need a finance manager," Olga informed him, wiping an invisible smudge from the Eldorado's flawless silver finish. "I'll be back in a day or two with the cash."

Before Dario could decide how to bring up the touchy matter of a deposit, Phil Palermo came out of his office with a stack of posters. "Had two hundred of these printed up," he announced, handing one to Dario. "My beautiful niece," he explained to Olga, trying not to be distracted by her unusual physique. "I'm sure you are aware of her tragic disappearance."

"Oh, yes," Olga replied, doing her best to sound concerned. "What a terrible story."

Dario was speechless as he studied the picture of his sister.

"She is my niece and this young man's sister," Phil explained to Olga. "That picture was taken at a cookout in my backyard just a few weeks ago. As lovely a young woman as you will ever meet." He rested the stack of posters on the trunk of the Eldorado while he unfolded a handkerchief and dabbed his eyes.

Lovely is right, Olga thought. *If I thought it would get there in time, I'd send Lester one of those posters so he could see what he is getting.*

"I'd like to get my hands on whoever took her," Dario said, finding his voice. "Give me five minutes in the same room with the bastard."

"As long as you leave something for me, Dario," his uncle added, taking a handful of posters from the pile.

Five minutes? Olga laughed silently with the most serious face she could manage. *Give me one minute with you two clowns, and I'll bend you into human pretzels.*

"Take these, Dario," his uncle told him, handing him the posters. "Bring them to the firehouse with you tomorrow and ask the guys to spread them around. I'm going to drop one off at every business in town."

Dario had been so absorbed with the beautiful picture of his sister that he had not noticed the bold letters at the bottom of the poster announcing a five-thousand-dollar reward for information leading to her return.

"Thank you, Uncle Phil, from me and my family," he said softly when he did.

"Whoever took Rita has no idea what kind of family she comes from," Uncle Phil assured Dario as he handed Olga her own copy. "On the off chance that you see her," he explained.

Olga almost laughed out loud.

As Rita's eyes grew more accustomed to the dim light, the moving shadows with red eyes took shape. They were rats. Big, ugly rats, screeching and clawing at each other as they fought over boxes of Cracker Jacks they had dragged out of the shadows. She balled up the rotted newspapers littering the floor around the cot and bombarded the frenzied rodents with the accuracy of the high school shortstop she had once been, more to pass the time than in hopes of driving them away. She understood that she was the intruder in this hellhole, not them, and the most she could hope for was that they were confused enough by her presence to leave her alone when she made her way across the floor to use the toilet or grab a water bottle from the workbench against the far wall. The presence of the snack food and water bottles puzzled her. One guess was that they had been left here to keep her alive, but if so, alive for what? Why would Gorilla Woman, the name she had given her jailer, care about keeping her alive and not Patricia?

Rita closed her eyes and reached for her father's hand, remembering the many times he told her that as long as she believed in herself, she could do anything she had to do: learn to ride a two-wheel bicycle, drive in the winning run when the chips were down, and not only get into nursing school but finish at the top of her class. *I'm on my way,* she heard him say, *but if I don't get there in time, you are an Anselmo, and you know what to do.*

32

Mary Beth retrieved the morning newspaper from her front walk with no more intention of reading it than she had of turning on her radio or watching television. The last thing she needed right now was to see pictures of her two nurses highlighting the horrible assumption that it was only a matter of time before Rita met the same fate as her friend and workmate Patricia Dugan. Across the street, a garage door opened and Vito Anselmo backed down his long driveway in a company truck. Mary Beth didn't know if it was the proper thing to do under the circumstances, but she waved to Vito, and without his usual smile, he waved back. She watched him leave the neighborhood, knowing her pain could in no way compare with the grief and despair that Rita's family was experiencing. She had just thrown the newspaper into the recycling bin when she saw someone appear from behind the Anselmo house, hurry across their wide side yard, and disappear into the hedge at the edge of the Greenberg's property. It was Vito's father

Vincenzo, she was sure of that, and she knew exactly how he was going to spend his day. Three times since she had been ordered to stay away from the hospital, the old man had wandered through her yard, searching for his granddaughter.

The hospital board's decision to put her on leave—for her own good, they had gone out of their way to clarify—had made a painful situation unbearable. She needed to get up in the morning and get out of a house where since Wade died, positive thoughts were hard to come by. It was still her address, but it was no longer a home. She cooked in the kitchen and ate in the kitchen and went into rooms like the big master bedroom overlooking the backyard only when she had to. A cleaning crew that she needed like a hole in the head still came once a week, a mother and a daughter who had worked for her and Wade for so long that she didn't have the heart to let them go. It was time to move on. She knew that and so should a certain man who seemed to be deaf, dumb, and blind to hints that had become anything but subtle.

Mary Beth went out onto the patio, hoping to find something to keep her mind occupied. The overnight rain had topped off the birdbath and watered the flowerpots, eliminating a chore that might have occupied fifteen minutes. The lawn looked perfect, thanks to the same people who did the Anselmo's yard, an arrangement made when Wade died that Vito insisted didn't cost him enough to worry about. She set her coffee on the wrought iron table and went into Wade's tool shed, a steep-roofed Hansel and Gretel affair he built himself on weekends, a project that took approximately the same amount of time it took the Egyptians to build the pyramids. Inside, on the same nail where Wade always hung it, Mary Beth found the old towel he used to dry the patio furniture. That task took all of five minutes, even after she stretched it out by wiping all four chairs, not just the one she settled into while opening a book she was trying to get into. The story was set in Venice, one of the many places she and Wade had always meant to visit. She found her place and read until it dawned on her that the beautiful American tourist she liked so much was about to be kidnapped. She let the book drop onto the patio and stared up into the big trees, struggling to focus on something, anything, less painful than thoughts of Rita and Patricia.

Focusing on Dr. Landau and his idiotic decision to place her on what he termed a mental health vacation was as good a distraction as any. "Damn his stupid ass," she swore passionately enough to scatter a small army of sparrows fighting for splash time in the birdbath.

Circumstances that were difficult for Mary Beth to imagine had forced Gregory R. Landau MD, the chief mental health specialist at St. Joseph's Memorial, to find his way down to the hospital cafeteria and fix his own cup of coffee. Standing behind him in the cash register line, Mary Beth wished him good morning in what she considered a perfectly normal tone of voice. He turned, raising his bushy eyebrows when he recognized her. "How are you dealing with…" He waved his free hand, apparently searching for the appropriate words. "With all that is going on?" is what he came up with.

"Oh, you know, I was going to take the elevator up to the roof and jump off but decided why go to all that trouble when I can just as easily poison myself to death with the god-awful concoction this hospital calls coffee?"

It was a dumb thing to say, especially to a man with the demeanor of a Bassett Hound, but she was tired of answering the same question and assumed that anyone with a brain larger than a walnut would realize that she was joking. Whatever the size of his brain, Dr. Landau was known to have difficulty recognizing humor, an affliction that proved accurate when he rubbed his chin and said, "Hmmm."

The ax dropped just before lunchtime when Mary Beth's email pinged.

The Hospital Board is in agreement with my conclusion that it is in the best interests of you personally and Saint Joseph's Memorial Hospital as an institu-

tion to direct you to take adequate time away from your professional responsibilities in order to rest and recuperate from the inevitable psychological effects of losing two of your nurses in such a shocking and traumatic manner. The Board has authorized me to state that you will be fully compensated for all such leave time, which is to commence immediately.

Gregory R. Landau MD,
Chief, Department of Mental Health and Wellness,
Saint Joseph's Memorial Hospital

It was like being sent home from school and told to stay there until she was all better. The problem was that she would never be *all better*. No one who knew Patricia and Rita as well as Mary Beth did ever would be.

Mary Beth glanced at her watch. It was nine in the morning. In normal times—meaning until ten days ago—Patricia and Rita would be getting off the hospital elevator with coffee from the Old Line Diner and, if it was their turn, a dozen bagels to share with the general surgical staff. Scenes like that were simply a part of life, unrecorded and unremarkable, but how unreal and special they now seemed, like the uncounted evenings when Wade came home from his office and sat here on the patio with his newspaper and his scotch. Life with a man like Wade Banakowski was not the way she had dreamed of spending her days, but it was the path she had taken, and at the end of those days, she had been left with this huge place and enough money to motivate Wade's financial advisor to call her at least once a week and suggest that they meet to discuss what he referred to as her positions in the market.

Mary Beth studied the ivied walls and dark green shutters of the big house that Wade had taken so much pride in owning. She knew what her position was, and it didn't have a damn thing to do with the stock market. She was lonely, and now, more than ever, she realized that nothing people care about lasts forever. Last night, alone in bed, was not the first time she'd thought about selling the house, but it was the first time she had asked herself what she was waiting for.

It suddenly dawned on Mary Beth that the leave of absence Dr. Landau sentenced her to was a blessing in disguise. She would use the time to get organized and make a few calls. A realtor. A mover. Someone to buy most of the furniture. Most of it, not all of it, she decided as she went into the house and walked from room to room. The place she was moving into needed furniture for the living room and dining room. She had yet to see the upstairs, but her guess was that it needed a woman's touch. In the kitchen, she found a notepad and made a list of what she would be taking with her. There was the little matter of letting her new roommate know what was going on, but there was no need to write herself a note about that. She would draw him a picture when she saw him tonight.

33

Lester Turner eased the van out of a garage as impressive as any luxury car showroom and sped to the end of the estate's winding drive where he stopped only long enough to activate the security gate and adjust his sunglasses. He was more excited than he had been in years. While watching the gate disappear into the boxwood hedge whose job it was to disguise the property's prison-like fencing, he congratulated himself once more for having the imagination to disguise the van as an ambulance. Who would stop an emergency vehicle on the road for speeding? he scoffed smugly. Who would look inside and question the presence of a cot with arm and leg straps or the need for a portable toilet? The wide red cross on both sides of the white van said it all. "Out of my way!" he sang out as the gate slid closed behind him. "A beautiful Italian Princess awaits!"

As he drove away from the lake and headed south, he wondered what nationality the last girl had been. Scandinavian, maybe. He wasn't sure.

Rita climbed the steep stairs and tried the cellar door again. It wouldn't budge, a discovery that, since it had also refused to budge the first four times, did not surprise her. She sat on the top step, remembering the old saying that trying the same thing over and over again and expecting a different result was a sign of stupidity or insanity. She laughed quietly when for the umpteenth time, she looked at her wrist to check the watch she had been unable to find in the dark mess surrounding the cot.

She was strangely calm, a blessing psychiatrists might have attributed to her child-like belief that her father Vito was going to appear any minute, kick down the door, and take her home. She leaned her head back against the door, closed her eyes, and concentrated on remaining positive. The trick that worked best was picturing herself at the dining room table with her family. Her father was at the end closest to the living room, and her mother was at the end near the kitchen, ready, as always, to jump up and get anything anyone needed. Her two brothers sat between her and her mother, facing the three grandparents who had lived with them as long as she could remember. Rita smiled, remembering the rules her mother laid down when Anthony and Dario moved out of the house. They were expected to eat dinner with the family every Sunday, on Christmas Day, and on Easter Sunday. No excuses. Family birthdays were originally included but were eliminated when Dario announced his intention to become a fire department paramedic rather than join the family business, a decision that meant he would sometimes work nights. Dario's second job, selling Cadillacs for their uncle Phil, did not come with a dinner pass. Marie Anselmo referred to her dinner rules as the Twelfth Commandment. The Eleventh Commandment dictated that both Dario and Anthony were to marry nice Italian girls, a subject raised at the table much too often to suit either one of them.

Rita stood, stretched, and started down the stairs, setting off squeals of protest from the creatures with red eyes. She was hungry and thirsty. The rats had devoured the remaining Cracker Jacks that had been left on the workbench but shown no interest in the bottles of water. Rita had taken three on her only trip across the dark floor and wished now that she had taken the other three. She clapped her hands and screamed one of her grandmothers' Italian curses to scatter the rats but had only taken a few nervous steps when she spotted what looked like a tool on top of the boiler. Using the cot as a stepstool, Rita pulled the object through a trail of cobwebs and dust and held it in her hands like a club. Most people would have called it a monkey wrench, but being the daughter of a man who owned a million tools, Rita knew better.

It was a pipe wrench, a very large pipe wrench. Its jaws were rusted shut, but that didn't matter. It was heavy, it was hard, and it was perfect. She turned and looked up the stairs. If Gorilla Woman came through that door before her father did, Rita would be ready for her.

Her Orioles jacket seemed to volunteer when Rita looked around for a place to hide the wrench. She pushed it into one of the sleeves. *The right sleeve,* she told herself. *Remember that, the right sleeve.* A rat the size of a cat sprinted from behind the cot and vanished under the boiler. It startled Rita but not enough to distract her from focusing on how surprised that horrible woman was going to be when she realized too late that she was not dealing with a lamb like Patricia.

34

Since Rita's disappearance, the once-joyful gatherings around the Anselmo family table had become unbearable occasions dominated by the painful presence of Rita's empty chair. Nonna Giovanna, Vito's mother, was the first to take her meals in the kitchen, a departure from tradition quickly adopted by the entire family. To keep busy, Rita's mother Maria cooked more than ever. "I'll go crazy if I sit still," she explained to her own mother Nana Nuncio, dabbing tears with the tip of an apron.

"Sit. Pray," Nana Nuncio told her. "I cook."

Maria handed the long wooden spoon to her mother and collapsed into a chair at the kitchen table. She thought about praying to Saint Jude, but it was much too painful to think of Rita's return as an impossible case, Saint Jude's specialty. She turned her attention to Saint Francis of Assisi, her favorite saint, whose small concrete statue held a place of honor in her tomato garden. Because it had never been entirely clear to her whether saints could see down from heaven, Maria had just begun to explain to Saint Francis that Rita had not yet been found when the smell of burning sauce opened her eyes to the sight of Nana Nuncio staring out the window. Maria slipped the spoon from her mother's hand, recognizing her almost inaudible Italian words as prayers for God to place His arms around Rita and bring her safely home.

Vito, watching from the kitchen door, felt completely helpless. He had searched every corner of the county, driven roads he had not known existed, and lost his temper with good people like T.J. Barnes who were doing everything they could to find his daughter. He was worried about his family. His sons Anthony and Dario were young and strong, but the others, especially his father Vincenzo, appeared to be on the edge of insanity. He went into the kitchen, put his arms around the two women, and held them tight. "I have to go to the office for a little while," he told them. "God will bring her home soon," he added, trying with all his heart to believe his own words.

Minutes after Vito left, his father, Vincenzo, slipped out of the house to resume his search for Rita, roaming the neighbors' neat summertime yards and peering into the cars parked in their long driveways. He cut across his son's property and squeezed through the hedge at the edge of the Greenbergs' property. Rina

Greenberg, talking on the telephone while sitting on her glass-walled sun porch, watched the old man's progress without alarm. She knew what he was doing and felt sorry for him. With two daughters of her own, she found it impossible to imagine what the Anselmo family was going through.

"That poor old man is at it again," she said into the telephone, lowering her voice as though she were doing the play-by-play at a golf match. "The first thing he will do is look behind every piece of shrubbery in our yard, then start peering into every window low enough for him to see through."

"Oh, no. I wouldn't think of calling the police," she replied after a few seconds of silence. "Some of the other neighbors did at first but backed off when they realized what he was doing. That and the fact that he is not all the way there if you know what I mean."

She stood, moved over to the glass wall, and craned her neck in the direction of her front yard, trying to keep track of Vincenzo's movements. "He's disappeared around the corner of the house," she said into the phone. "The last thing he will do before moving on is peer through the windows of my Escalade. It's so sad to watch."

The old man worked his way down the street, searching places he had searched a dozen times before. At the end of the block, he watched two deliverymen unload a new refrigerator and roll it up a flagstone walk while Elaine Shapiro, one of Marie Anselmo's best friends, held the door open for them. As Vincenzo watched, a figure with long, black hair passed through the hallway behind Mrs. Shapiro.

"Rita, Bambina! Rita, Bellissima Bambina!" Vincenzo screamed, hurrying up the walk as fast as his tired legs would carry him. He squeezed past the two deliverymen wrestling with the crated refrigerator and ignored Mrs. Shapiro's outstretched arms.

"Mr. Anselmo…!"

Breathing hard, the old man looked around in confusion. Seeing that the rooms on both sides of the hallway were empty, he continued into the kitchen where the Shapiros' son, David, was searching for his Grateful Dead coffee mug.

"Rita, Bambina!" Vincenzo screamed frantically.

David Shapiro, who had dropped out of Georgetown after one semester to form a rock band named The Peeved Frogs, dropped the Grateful Dead mug into the sink, snapping off the handle. "Goddamn it!" he howled, spinning around so fast that his long black hair half covered his face before coming to rest on his shoulders.

The sight of David Shapiro's scraggly beard and nose ring dumbfounded Vincenzo Anselmo. He started backing out of the kitchen with his mouth open just as Mrs. Shapiro caught up with him.

"It's okay, David," she said to her son. "You stay here while these two gentlemen install the new refrigerator. I'm going to take Mr. Anselmo home."

The Carnival

"Somebody owes me a new Grateful Dead coffee mug!" David Shapiro called after his mother. "Those things don't grow on trees, you know!"

That night, too tired to do anything else, Vito spent time with his daughter's pictures. From the ones taken when she was a baby to the portrait of her with her brothers made the previous Easter, there were photographs of Rita in every room of the house. Marie, who could no longer bear to look at them, wanted to take them down and put them away, but Vito wouldn't let her. With the thousand memories locked forever in his heart, every picture, large or small, formed a precious connection to his lost daughter.

On the desk in his home office, there was a framed snapshot of a very young Rita dressed like a cowgirl. Vito took it in his hands, remembering how, on that long-ago Halloween, Marie wanted Rita to wear a princess costume, and Rita refused, insisting that she wanted to be a racecar driver, goggles and all, or an astronaut with a space suit and a laser gun. In the end, she reluctantly agreed to wear a cowgirl outfit that Marie proposed as a compromise. On one condition, Vito remembered with the beginning of a smile. Rita would go trick-or-treating dressed as a cowgirl only if she was allowed to carry two pistols loaded with real caps.

Vito checked to make sure his father Vincenzo, was sleeping, then slipped into the bedroom to check on Marie. As he watched, she moved restlessly and made soft sounds that were almost words. It wasn't perfect sleep, but it was sleep she badly needed. On his way back down the hallway, he stopped and leaned his head against Rita's bedroom door. *Bring her back to me, God, please bring her back,* he prayed as tears filled his eyes for the first time since his mother died. Desperation and anger knotted into a single emotion so overwhelming that he began to shake. *What kind of people do such horrible things?* he cried silently, slipping to the floor and dropping his face into his hands. *Don't they understand what it means to love another human being? Don't they know that family is the only thing in life that really matters?* His love for one person was wrapped in hate for another that had grown beyond control.

In the kitchen, Vito poured a glass of red wine, drank it slowly, and resisted a strong temptation to have a second. He went into the den, fell into his old leather chair, and picked up the framed photograph that he had held in his hands for what seemed like hours the night before. It was a picture of Rita, posing in the batting stance she stubbornly refused to let her brothers tinker with. Her raven hair was tied back in a ponytail. Black grease was smeared under her eyes in imitation of the major leaguers she followed religiously on television and at Camden Yards. Rita stared past the camera at an imaginary pitcher, daring her to throw the ball over the plate. *That was exactly the way she faced life,* Vito thought to himself, as tears formed in his eyes again. "God bless Rita, and God help whoever took her," he whispered hoarsely. It wasn't the prayer of a saint, but it was the best he could do.

35

"I'm in the living room," Mary Beth called when she heard T.J. open the back door.

He took off his hat and gun, pulled a beer from the refrigerator, and dragged himself into the living room where she was sitting with her back against the wall.

"Pull up a chair," she said with a smile, patting the floor next to her.

He did, squeezing past the weightlifting equipment in the middle of the room. "I've been meaning to get some furniture," he said.

"We have to talk about that."

The way she said it made T.J. pause with the cold beer halfway to his lips. "Excuse me?" he asked warily.

"We'll get back to that. First, tell me about your day. Any news about Rita?"

T.J. took a long swallow, and then another, before shaking his head. "Lots of looking, lots of phone calls, and more tips that led nowhere."

"Like?"

THE CARNIVAL

"Like the driver for Wayne's Pizza who told us he was making a delivery to an RV parked near the bridge out on Reservoir Road when a girl bolted out of the door, knocking a pepperoni pizza and an order of wings out of his hands. A second later, a man wearing nothing but a pair of boxer shorts stormed out of the RV and chased her into the woods down near the creek. The pizza driver said he called because the girl looked exactly like the picture of the missing nurse they've been showing on TV."

"But it wasn't," Mary Beth concluded quietly.

"It wasn't, but it was a good thing the driver had the sense to get in touch with us." He took another swig and a deep breath. "Because two months ago, the RV woman, who is the same age as Rita Anselmo, was forced into a car outside a shopping mall in North Carolina by a man she had filed a restraining order against."

"The guy in the boxer shorts?"

T.J. nodded. "Two of Duke Cumberland's men caught up with him and pulled him out of Cattail Creek."

Mary Beth bit her lip. It would have been fine with her if the two troopers had let a bastard like that drown, but saying so would have triggered T.J.'s well-honed homily about people taking the law into their own hands. He was unmovable on the subject, and pointing out to him that one lovely young woman in his county had been brutally murdered and, for all he knew, another may have suffered the same horrible fate wasn't going to change his thinking. She started to get up and finish getting dinner ready when T.J. said something that made her wonder if he somehow sensed the bombshell she planned to lay on him after she had fortified him with a good meal.

"When I have time to think about it, I'm going to look for some furniture for this room and maybe get something for the dining room. I was hoping you could help me pick it out."

"That won't be necessary," she said, deciding this was as good a time as any to get on with it. "I've already picked it out."

A very long day had affected T.J.'s ability to understand what Mary Beth had just said or to sense that the subject of furniture was only incidental to the bomb she was about to drop.

"I put my house on the market," Mary Beth opened with. "You and I are going to have more furniture than we will ever need."

T.J. studied the empty beer bottle, wondering if he was losing his tolerance for alcohol. "Run that by me again," he said warily.

"My house in Country Club Estates is on the market. I spoke with the realtor today. There will be a sign in the front yard tomorrow."

It took a minute for T.J. to absorb this information and come to the wrong conclusion. "Moving into a smaller place?" he asked.

"That's my plan."

"You mean like one of those townhouses they're building out on River Road?"

She shook her head.

T.J. had just begun to wonder if he was supposed to make another guess when distant alarm bells went off. He pushed to his feet and stared through the window at the street of modest houses where he had lived since he was a boy. His roots were here, and unlike Mary Beth, he could not imagine moving. It would be like growing a beard or having his ears pierced. There was nothing wrong with doing things like that, but if he did them, he wouldn't feel like the same person. Mary Beth came up behind him and put her arms around his waist, something she had not done since they lived in another world. "Chief Barnes," she announced softly, "you are going to have a roommate."

The house was very quiet as they walked into the kitchen. "You can marry me or not marry me," Mary Beth informed him as she unfolded her napkin, "but I'm going to spend the rest of my life right here with you. I lost you once, and then I lost Wade, and now I've seen poor Patricia's life cut short and...." She began to cry when her thoughts turned to Rita.

T.J. reached across the table and took her hand. Another man might have known what to say, but he didn't, a shortcoming that had become obvious when they were in high school.

36

Hints of bright neon appeared and disappeared through the stands of pine bordering the road before revealing themselves as a sign mounted to the roof of a roadside bar. It did not appear to be the type of establishment he normally frequented, but it would do quite well, Lester decided, for placing a telephone call and enjoying a libation or two to celebrate his arrival.

"Where are you?" Olga asked.

Lester leaned close to the windshield and looked up at the sign. "At a quaint tavern known as the Starlight Lounge," he informed her. "I believe I can detect the roar of happy patrons all the way out here in the parking lot."

There was a minute of silence before Olga remembered that she had dropped off a stack of posters at the Starlight Lounge the day the carnival rolled into town. "That's perfect," she said into her cellphone as she slipped into a narrow opening between the cotton candy trailer and the goldfish toss. "Stay where you are. I'll meet you there and lead you to the church as soon as I can get away."

"The church? Yes, of course. You mentioned that quaint detail the last time we spoke."

Olga was about to repeat to Lester that she wanted him to stay where he was when Dotty Green, who was supposed to be manning the popcorn stand, spotted Olga and hurried over to her. "That fireman guy Jerry is mad as hell," she said breathlessly. "It's almost time for the motorcycle raffle and he can't get his microphone to work."

With a bundle of Lester's money about to make her a rich woman, Olga no longer gave a damn about fire chiefs or their microphones. Putting a hand over the phone, she told Dotty to get back to the popcorn stand before she kicked her ass.

"Where were we, Lester? Oh, yes. Stay right where you are. I'll get there as soon as I can."

"My dear Olga, I remain curious about your ingenious use of a church."

Olga glanced toward the goldfish toss to make sure no one was listening. "It's just an old building with a steeple that has been abandoned so long that cobwebs are the only thing holding it up. The pretty little thing I found for you is locked in the cellar."

"Like a princess in a dungeon," Lester mused excitedly. "Tell me where the young damsel awaits so I can dash over there and become acquainted with her while I await your arrival."

"It's on Woodyard Road between a railroad crossing and Michele's Florists," Olga whispered into her cell phone as she spotted an angry Jerry Donnelly searching the crowd for her. "But, Lester, stay where you are. As soon as I can get away from this zoo, I'll meet you and take you to her. By the way, what are you driving?"

Lester told her, describing with schoolboy pride the white ambulance with big red crosses on both sides.

"An ambulance?" Olga thought about that for a second and shrugged her big shoulders. "Whatever."

In the dark church cellar, the rats grew bolder by the day, creeping from hiding places and gathering in shadowy bunches to glare at Rita with their red eyes and squeal protests at her continued presence. She was tired and hungry, but she was not afraid, not of a bunch of rats or the strange woman who held her prisoner. Stay brave, she kept telling herself, just stay brave and either her father would come crashing through the door at the top of the stairs or she would do what she had to do and bash Gorilla Woman's head in with the pipe wrench that was hidden in her jacket. The woman was a murderer, finding Patricia's clothes was proof enough of that, and Rita had no intention of having the same thing happen to her.

An old memory made her smile. When she was a little girl, her grandfather Vincenzo had loved to laugh and call her his *biscotto duro*, his tough cookie. When this nightmare was over, she would remind him about that.

Rita concentrated, going over the plan one more time. The second she saw the woman start down the stairs, she would close her eyes and pretend she was asleep. The Orioles jacket would be spread over her like a blanket, and the pipe wrench would be in her hand just like it was now. Like taking batting practice, she threw the jacket aside and swung the wrench in the air as hard as she could. Rats squealed and scattered. One swing might be all she was going to get, so it had to be a good one. With little red eyes staring at her from every corner of the cellar, she swung the wrench again and again.

37

By Lester's count, half the vehicles parked in the Starlight's unpaved lot were pickup trucks or work vans. The others were motorcycles, bunched together near the propped-open door like a herd of horses awaiting the return of their riders. The big neon sign on the roof flickered like a dying light fixture. The effect of bright colors pulsing against a dark sky reminded Lester of fireworks he had seen at the Carnival in Rio de Janeiro, an interpretation, he was certain, that had never occurred to the owners of these vehicles. No doubt he could find a more suitable establishment in which to unwind after such a long day on the road, but Olga had instructed him to wait for her here, so, he told himself, unbuckling his seat belt, that was exactly what he was going to do. The trash barrel next to the front door overflowed with more beer cans than Lester had emptied in his entire life. He was a scotch man himself, Port Ellen-forty-year-old if available, Macallan in a pinch. As Lester excused himself through the shoulder-to-shoulder crowd inside the door, he decided his need for rejuvenation was such that he might even settle for a Johnnie Walker Black.

The barmaid tossed a beer-soaked towel over her shoulder and lit a cigarette. "Never heard of any of them," she said. "All I have is what you see lined up at the mirror behind me."

Lester saw no Port Ellen or Macallan; in fact, he saw no scotch. "When in Rome," he smiled.

Renee, the barmaid, flicked ashes onto the bar and wiped them away with her hand. "You are not in Rome, darling. You are in Hargrove, Maryland," she informed him.

"A trite expression of resignation, my dear lady. Let me have a double of your best bourbon."

Renee placed her cigarette in a line of burn marks at the edge of the bar and measured the pour with one open eye. "Kentucky Gentleman double. Eight dollars."

Lester slipped into an empty booth next to the front door and raised his glass. "To you, my Good Lady, and to the untold pleasures that await Yours Truly upon the completion of this little road trip."

"I don't know what the hell you are talking about, but that booth belongs to The Road Dogs, and they expect to find it empty when they get here."

"I shan't be long," he informed Renee as she hustled past him with the necks of six beer bottles locked between her fingers.

"It's your ass," she informed him.

After an initial shock to his system, the fiery bourbon worked its way into Lester's road-weary muscles and set fire to fantasies starring the unspoiled maiden who was about to be delivered to him. Lester checked his Rolex, hoping Olga would not be long. He waved his empty glass at Renee.

She delivered the second double with the information that no one in their right mind wanted to be sitting in their booth when The Road Dogs showed up. "I've seen people make that mistake," she informed him, flicking ash from her cigarette. "It wasn't pretty."

Lester slid a ten and then a twenty across the table, the biggest tip in the history of the Starlight Lounge. "A nubile maiden awaits," he announced raising his glass.

Because they were the only kind of women the men who drank at the Starlight found interesting, Renee interpreted nubile as meaning ready, willing, and able. "You horny old devil," she laughed.

"I beg your pardon, Madam," Lester replied with slightly slurred indignation as the second double began to kick in. He stood uncertainly. The centerpiece of *Italian Princess Night*, a little surprise he planned for his special friends back home, awaited. In an old church of all places. He described the location to Renee.

"Yeah. Between the railroad tracks and the florist shop. Woodyard Road. You got a little action waiting for you in that old church?"

Lester put a finger to his lips. "Is it far?" he asked.

For another ten dollars, Renee told him the best way to get to the church.

Lester made his way unsteadily to the van, so distracted by the anticipation of taking possession of his beautiful princess that he was unaware of the heavy raindrops announcing the arrival of a storm. "Take a right out of the parking lot," he told himself as he searched for the windshield wiper controls. "Just past the railroad tracks." Between swipes of the wiper blades, he wondered whether it was the long day of driving or the unfamiliar bourbon that made staying on his side of the yellow lines such a puzzling game.

Before his taillights disappeared around the first bend, the Road Dogs roared out of the rain and splashed into the Starlight parking lot. All of them were big. Some had guts but the others were as fit as prize fighters. Three had shaved heads, and three wore doo rags and ponytails. On the way to the door, they kicked over the half-dozen motorcycles that had dared park in their spaces. Inside, they stomped water from their boots and shook rain from their leather jackets like wet animals.

"You boys hear anything about a whore house opening on Woodyard Road?" Renee asked as she slid three pitchers of beer onto their table.

Marty Funk, the biggest of the bunch, dried his hands on his doo rag before returning it to his head. "A good whore house is what this uptight county needs," he declared, drinking straight from the pitcher. "Why? You hear something, Renee?"

"There was this funny little guy in here; you must have just missed him in the parking lot. Anyway, he got half-bombed on two bourbons and let it slip that there was action to be had in that old church between the railroad crossing and the florist shop."

They looked at each other, grinning through beards and broken teeth. "Well, boys," Marty bellowed, raising the pitcher, "what say we drink up and go to church?"

38

It wasn't the bourbon, Lester decided, it was the lousy job some idiot had done painting the center line. Everyone knew it was supposed to stay in the middle of the road, not wander from side to side like a long yellow snake. He narrowed his eyes and tried to concentrate on the road while visions of a triumphant return to his mansion bearing an unspoiled maiden fought for his attention. How excited his friends were going to be when they laid eyes on her young body and drew cards to determine who would go first. The contemplation of such a glorious homecoming was so intoxicating that Lester did not notice when the yellow line moved again. Blinding headlights and blaring horns swept past him and vanished into the wet night. A second later, tree branches whipped the side of the van, confusing him. He rolled down the window and slapped his face. *It can't be much farther,* he told himself, fighting his way back onto the road.

A sober man would have heard the warning blasts of the freight train approaching the Woodyard Road crossing. Lester was no more aware of what sounded like rolling thunder than he was of the rain-blurred lights of the motorcycles filling his rearview mirror. His faltering attention was focused on trying to remember what time Olga was supposed to meet him at the church. As he pushed the Rolex free of his sleeve and pulled it close to his nose, the red lights of the crossing gate flashed red. He never saw the lights, and he never heard the bells. The Road Dogs, riding his rear bumper, squeezed brake levers hard and slid to a stop. The ground shook as the massive locomotive roared out of the night. A thunderous blast of its whistle panicked Lester. His mouth opened but his foot never made it to the brake pedal. Mangled steel and engine parts showered the night.

Investigators determined later that only 85 percent of the demolished van had been located. The remains of the driver were pieced together at the county morgue like a medical school exercise. One of the van's tires rolled a half-mile down the road before hitting the base of a billboard heralding the return of the firemen's carnival. Money flew everywhere, tens, twenties, and fifties that would be hunted like Easter eggs for years. Three weeks after the wreck, a scrupulously honest couple picking wild raspberries fifty yards from the tracks found a battered alligator skin valise with forty-three thousand dollars still strapped into it.

The Carnival

The collision triggered ground waves powerful enough to rock the foundations of the old church, showering the cellar with dust from a thousand cracks and crevices and startling Rita from a dream that had taken her home. Her father opened the door and led her inside where tears and kisses and prayers of thanksgiving filled the house. Her mother had just hurried into the kitchen to get her something to eat when noise and confusion returned her to the darkness of reality. As she struggled to sit up, the wailing of sirens filled her with the hope that someone had found out where she was, the police were coming to rescue her, and any minute now, she would be free.

Still groggy from sleep, she made it to the foot of the stairs and put her hands on the railing. The nightmare was almost over. When the police stormed into the church, she would call out to them through the cellar door so they could find her and take her home. She climbed to the top and sat, waiting. The aroma of Italian food that had spiced the dream returned and made her smile.

39

Storm clouds slipped into place above the carnival grounds, threatening to send the final-night crowd running for cover before the motorcycle raffle put an official end to the two-week run. Olga Muntz saw the building clouds and laughed. She was about to become a rich woman, and after that, the skies could empty, tents could be blown away, and every deadbeat on her payroll could start looking for someone else to rob blind. Visions of sliding behind the wheel of a beautiful Eldorado were interrupted by the wailing whistle of the nightly freight train followed by an earth-shaking rumble that she assumed was thunder. "Bring it on," she told the dark sky. "Hit me with your best shot."

Olga's cell phone rang while she was watching the popcorn stand, trying to decide whether LaVerne Hooks was tying her shoe or slipping a couple of ones into her sock. "Going to be late getting there," John Bullman, her night watchman, announced on the phone. "I'm stuck in a line of traffic that ain't going anywhere."

Keeping her eyes on LaVerne, Olga told him to cut the bullshit.

"I ain't kidding. I saw the whole thing. White ambulance ran through the railroad crossing on Woodyard Road. Lights flashing, bells ringing, the whole nine yards. Big ass train crushed that sucker like a grape."

Olga assumed she was being fed a strangely elaborate excuse by one of her few honest employees and was about to tell him he better get his ass to the carnival when a certain detail of his story hit home.

"Did you say a white ambulance?"

"White with big red crosses on the sides. But that ain't the coolest thing. That ambulance must have been hauling some damned billionaire because when the train hit it, money flew all over the place. A bunch of bikers went crazy stuffing bills in their jacket pockets until the cops got there and chased them away. I grabbed a couple of twenties and some tens that landed on my windshield."

Olga hung up while the man was still talking and dialed Lester's cellphone number. The muscles in her wide shoulders tightened with each ring.

As the final hour of the Hargrove Volunteer Fire Department carnival ticked away, Chief Jerry Donnelly stepped onto the stage to take one last crack at selling raffle tickets. He was halfway through his pitch when the sky opened, drenching him to the skin and shorting out his microphone again. "Find the damn woman who runs this carnival and get her over here to fix this mic!" he shouted to one of his men as potential customers ran for the parking lot. "You've seen her. She looks like a weightlifter."

The description did not help. Olga was long gone.

From the dark recess of the church entrance, Olga fixed her eyes on the small army of emergency vehicles crowding the railroad crossing at the bottom of the hill. Two rain-blurred caboose lamps were the only signs of the train that had dragged the wreckage of Lester's van, and what was left of him, far down the tracks and out of sight. Her thoughts were not on Lester Turner or the gruesome way his pampered life had ended. All she could think about was all that money—her money—blowing like trash through the wet grass and trees along the tracks where it would be pocketed by stampeding fortune hunters the minute the police lines came down. She unleashed a stream of obscenities that were lost in the mocking chatter of distant police radios.

Olga's shaking hands felt through her pockets for the key to the church. The nurse in the cellar was now as worthless to her as the first one had been, she told herself. There was nothing to do but get rid of her.

The Carnival

Rita heard the footsteps. It could be her father coming to rescue her, but if it wasn't, she was ready. Returning quietly to the cot, she pulled the Orioles jacket into her lap and felt for the wrench. More footsteps and then silence. Closing her eyes, she prayed for the strength to do what she had to do.

40

The lines of empty pews sat black against the gray nothingness of the empty church. Using her strong hands to guide her, Olga inched her way to the last row and sat down. She was dangerously angry but smart enough to know it. Before doing anything stupid, she needed to think. She wasn't used to being flat on her back, but thanks to Lester's brilliant idea to play a game of chicken with a freight train, she was there now. The money was gone, scattered like leaves to be raked up by greedy nitwits or dragged away by animals to paper their dens and lairs. None of it would ever be hers, not one wrinkled dollar.

With the distant emergency lights pulsing red in the church windows, Olga was struck with the sickening realization that she was thinking like a loser. She felt herself pushing up onto one knee, then reaching for the ring ropes and rising to her feet. Her head began to clear. Downstairs in a rat-infested cellar, there was a beautiful young girl who had to be worth plenty of money to someone. Someone who would pay through the nose to get her back. Feeling her way toward the cellar door, she thought about the taunting high school cheerleaders and their rich families, the Mercedes that picked them up after school, the country clubs where they tanned their skinny asses. All their parents had money, and Olga was willing to bet the family of the girl downstairs either had it or would do whatever it took to get it. She slipped the cellar door key from her pocket. There was a lot of work to do before this night was over, but she was on her feet again, and she was going to win. She could hear the crowd chanting her name.

When the lock at the top of the stairs rattled, Rita prayed that she would hear her father call her name. Heavy footsteps on the steep stairs became the shape and then the voice of Gorilla Woman. "Time to talk, Girl," it announced.

Rita slipped the wrench halfway out of the jacket. The woman's voice was powerful and intimidating. "We need to talk about your family."

Rita said nothing, watching and waiting for her chance.

"Is your Daddy rich?"

A second later, the same words exploded in anger. "I said, is your Daddy rich?"

Rita had never thought much about it. She supposed he was rich enough. They lived in a big house. He gave a lot of money to the church, like when he built the grotto. "I guess he is," Rita answered softly, trying to get the woman to come closer.

It was working. "What does he do?"

"He owns a construction company," Rita answered even more softly.

"A construction company. Now we are getting somewhere." Olga knew that contractors made a lot of money. Her hard heart was pounding.

Gorilla Woman was close enough for Rita to see that her clothes were wet. The realization was strangely uplifting. It was raining in the world outside, the world she was about to see again.

Olga wanted to know more. "What is your father's name?"

Rita did not want to tell the woman anything else about her family, but she needed her to come a little closer. "Vito Anselmo," she said, almost whispering as her hand tightened on the wrench.

"Speak up, goddamn you!" Olga screamed.

"Vito Anselmo!" Rita screamed back.

"And where…?"

Rita struck. "You killed my friend Patricia!" she screamed, swinging the wrench with every ounce of strength in her weary body.

Olga raised her left arm to block the blow, but she was a second too late. The pain in her elbow was excruciating. "You little bitch!" she roared.

Rita's head snapped back when Olga hit her the first time. She went out like a light when the second one landed. Olga jerked her off the cot and was about to hit Rita again when her brain muscled in. *With Lester dead,* she warned herself, *this girl you are about to beat to a pulp is the last chance you will ever have to get out of the carnival business; your last shot at taking off for Easy Street behind the wheel of a big-ass Cadillac.* Her mind raced. Her fist uncoiled. She made herself think. Did the girl have to be alive, or did her contractor father just have to believe that she was alive? Olga made her way back to the stairs and sat down, trying to think. The curious rats followed her with their red eyes. "Get the hell away from me!" she yelled, jumping back up and taking a few quick steps toward them. They retreated, squealing, to the far side of the cellar where they stopped and aimed their eyes at her again. "Filthy bastards," she swore, sitting back down. There wasn't much time to work out a plan. In the morning, she had a carnival to break down, pack up, and get on the road.

Olga Muntz had a way of pumping herself up when problems got in her way. She imagined herself in a foul-smelling, smoke-filled arena, climbing into the ring and coming face to face with an opponent she had never seen before: a real hard ass, she had been warned by the losers in the locker room, who was going to kick her ass all over the ring. Olga's mind cleared as she imagined herself slipping out of her robe, narrowing her eyes, and concentrating on what she had to do. Even if Mr. Contractor paid the ransom, it wouldn't make any sense to leave the girl in this rat-hole cellar and have someone find her, even if she was just a pile of bones by the time they did. The coat-and-tie realtor who rented her this place might not know Olga's name, but he knew what she looked like, and that was far too much information to leave behind. Killing the girl and dumping her like she dumped the other one was the only answer. Olga checked her mental notebook. Vito Anselmo was the father's name. He owned a construction company. It would be easy enough to find him in the phone book and send him the ransom note. Two hundred and fifty thousand dollars was what it would cost for him to believe he was going to get his precious little girl back. She snapped the book closed. It was a good plan. Even if the girl's father had to hock his trucks and bulldozers and everything else he owned, Olga was sure he would do it. Her own father would never have done it, but that was another story because he was a complete asshole and she was not a princess.

The rats retreated again when Olga stood up. This time, she didn't notice. The elbow where the girl had hit her hurt like hell. Standing over the cot, rubbing it, Olga started thinking about the kidnapping movies she had seen. She liked the way kidnappers made their ransom notes by cutting words out of newspapers. There were sharp scissors in her trailer but no newspaper and no note paper or envelopes without the name of the carnival printed all over them. Olga checked her watch. Drugstores stayed open late. Drugstores sold everything she needed. "Don't go anywhere, Princess," she laughed at Rita's limp body. "I'll be right back."

At the top of the stairs, Olga opened the door and heard the rain. Her jacket was soaked and, she suddenly realized, the name of her carnival was embroidered across the back for anyone at the drugstore to see and remember. There was a jacket on the cot next to the girl, an orange and black one with a picture of a stupid bird on the front. To Olga's amazement, it fit. It was a little snug in the shoulders, but it was good enough for a rainy night.

41

Vito Anselmo had searched every corner of the county, driven roads he had not known existed, and lost his temper with good people like T.J. Barnes who were doing everything they possibly could to find his daughter. Except for his two boys who were young and strong, his family had become sleepwalking zombies. When his father, Vincenzo, was not driving the neighbors crazy with his endless searches, he sat on the back porch mumbling prayers. The three women cooked and cleaned and broke out in tears when their eyes met.

For the first time in a week, Vito forced himself to go into the office and try to put a dent in the work that landed on his desk whether he was there or not. There were monthly requisitions to finalize, checks to sign, and a bid for the new county parking garage that Anthony wanted Vito to go over before he finalized it.

By the time he was done it was almost dark outside. He was about to climb into his truck when his cell phone rang.

"Hey, Dad, it's Anthony. Just wanted to let you know that the underground spring at the hospital plaza has been capped and tested, and we are scheduled to backfill the excavation with concrete at the crack of dawn Monday morning. Five ready-mix trucks loaded to the gills. No need for you to be there. Everything is under control."

Vito thanked his son and made an effort at small talk until the silences outnumbered the words and he told Anthony he would see him and Dario at Sunday dinner.

He remembered to stop outside the storage yard and lock the big double gate behind him but wasn't sure what to do next. It was Saturday night. Tomorrow after Mass, he would hit the road and drive all day looking for Rita. Tonight, as difficult as it would be, he knew he should go home and spend time with the family. Their evenings were no longer a time of peace and comfort, and the more the family tried to pretend they were, the longer and emptier the hours became. He slammed the truck door, thought it over, and made a decision. He would go home because it was the right thing to do, but first, he would head over to the hospital and satisfy himself that the plaza was ready for the tons of concrete Anthony had ordered. Concrete was Vito's business, and one thing he had learned the hard way was that before tons of it came rolling down the chute, every inch of formwork had to be strong and true, and the reinforcing bars had to be laid out with the exactness of quilt work. In his many years in the business, he had learned how to do everything except put concrete back into a truck.

A police officer T.J. Barnes had stationed outside the hospital recognized Vito and waved him through with a smile that Vito did not return. He felt like rolling down the window and asking where the hell the cops had been on the nights when that poor girl Patricia and his Rita walked out of the hospital and disappeared. Settling for a quiet curse, he moved aside a barricade and stepped inside the large circle of forms that would soon shape a concrete plaza as hard and permanent as solid rock. He walked across the gravel, stepping between carefully placed reinforcing bars until he stood at the edge of the excavation that had been required by the discovery of the underground spring. The hole Vito stared down into was a good six feet deep. At the bottom, he recognized the water collection box known as a French Drain that connected the spring to a newly installed storm line. In the fading light, Vito saw that the capping of the well was finally finished. He tossed a handful of gravel into the deep hole and listened to it hit bottom. The well-capping specialist, a strange bird from West Virginia who spent as much time talking about hunting dogs and squirrel stew as he did directing the work he was hired to do, had been fascinated by Vito's decision to fill the hole with solid concrete and remarked that if the Egyptians had thought like Vito Anselmo, their mummies would still be undiscovered.

As he made his way out of the work area, Vito was so distracted by the thought of someone lying under six feet of concrete until the end of time that he almost tripped over a long-handled shovel that one of his men had left on the ground. He threw it into the back of his truck and climbed behind the wheel. His head throbbed and his neck felt like it was tied in knots. He glanced at the dashboard clock. Marie would not be putting dinner on the table for almost an hour, a nightly routine that, for the first time since they were married, had become for her more of a duty than a joy. Theirs had become a table without laughter or familiar stories repeated with smiles, and if gathering for dinner had become a silent burden, the heavy hours after the meal were worse. Silent card games and half-watched television shows did little to mask the unrelenting drumbeat of nightmare thoughts that haunted them all.

The traffic light where he was sitting turned green and then yellow before Vito realized that the driver behind him was leaning on his horn.

Three blocks down the road, Vito turned into the CVS parking lot and found a space near the front door. He didn't notice the beat-up Ford Bronco parked next to him, and if he had, it would have meant nothing to him. A headache he managed to ignore all afternoon had become a screaming storm; his eyes hurt, his neck hurt, and he was starting to feel sick to his stomach. There was no way he could let himself go home feeling the way he did. He was supposed to be the strong one, the person his distraught wife and Rita's three bewildered grandparents crowded around the second he came through the door, desperate to hear from him that Rita had been found, that she was unharmed, and that the police would be bringing her home any minute.

Glaring rows of ceiling fixtures flooded the drugstore with light so bright that Vito had trouble focusing on the suspended signs announcing *Greeting Cards*, *Beauty Aids*, *Personal Care*, and *Pet Supplies*. Inflated balloons tethered to long ribbons called his attention to every product except the one he was looking for. "Come on, headache medicine, where the hell are you?" he mumbled, rubbing his temples.

As Vito made his way toward the rear of the store, he squeezed through an aisle stocked with what appeared to be every brand of candy known to man. He reached *Toys and Games* before stopping. Marie loved candy, the two grandmothers loved candy, and his father Vincenzo would eat a bucket of M&M's if someone didn't stop him. Bringing home a little candy was not going to make anyone forget the nightmare their lives had become, he told himself, but it sure as hell wouldn't hurt anything.

"Are you a baseball fan?" the woman behind the register asked Vito as he placed the Advil, two regular-size packs of M&M's, two Hershey bars, and a bag of miniature Peppermint Patties—Marie's favorites—on the counter.

Vito nodded, reaching for his wallet.

"Good, then let me ask you something: Were any of the Baltimore Orioles nicknamed 'Slugger?'"

Vito stared at her. "What?"

"A woman who was here just a minute ago was wearing an orange and black Orioles jacket with the name 'Slugger' stitched on it. I asked her what Oriole was nicknamed 'Slugger,' but she didn't answer me. She dumped a newspaper, a box of envelopes, and some note paper on the counter and wanted to know why we didn't carry cigarillos. When I told her that we didn't carry any smokes, she looked at me like she was going to punch me in the nose. Strange woman. Built like an ape."

Before she could begin ringing up Vito's pile of candy, he rushed outside. The only vehicle on the move had just forced itself into the Emerson Street traffic, leaving in its wake blaring horns and squealing brakes. It had to be the woman wearing Rita's jacket. There were no other vehicles in the parking lot with their lights on. The space where the old Bronco had been was empty. Vito slammed his truck into reverse, demolished a row of small shrubs as he cut across a parking island, and swerved out onto Emerson Street with his back tires squealing.

42

Car lights filled the wet night, waves of bright headlights half-blinding Vito as he concentrated on the two taillights he was chasing. He pulled closer to the Bronco, insanely determined to ram it from behind until it dawned on him that Rita, bound and gagged and possibly injured, might be inside. He dropped back, in time, he hoped, to keep from being noticed. His headache and aching neck were not even a memory. All that mattered was keeping the Bronco in sight.

The chase continued west until Emerson Street met Woodyard Road and the Bronco turned right. Vito knew the town like a book. Michele's Florists would be coming up on the left, then that old church. The only thing on the right side of Woodyard Road was an abandoned tobacco field where his boys hunted rabbits when they were young. There were no streetlights and, suddenly, no Bronco taillights. Vito pulled onto the shoulder and killed his own lights. At the bottom of the hill, flashing red and blue, emergency strobes lit the wet night. It was obvious that there had been an accident at the railroad crossing, but that was of no interest to Vito. He had lost the Bronco. With his truck dark and the windows open, he drifted slowly down the shoulder, looking and listening. Just as he was about to go mad at the thought of losing his chance to rescue Rita, he heard something in the distant darkness. The sound of a car door. Up near the old church.

Vito made himself wait. Another door sounded faintly. He counted to thirty, then sixty, and with waist-high weeds scraping the underside of the truck, crossed an abandoned parking lot until he spotted the Bronco's dark shape in front of the silent church. He reached for the work gloves on the seat next to him and put them on, an unthinking act for which he would forever be thankful.

The unlocked door of the church groaned as Vito pushed it open. Inside, nothing but shadows peopled the neat rows of pews. He debated going back to the truck for a flashlight but decided its bright beam might give his presence away. The moon, fighting its way through a breaking sky, lit the dusty windows just enough to reveal the presence of a door in a far corner. He moved slowly across the creaking floor and carefully turned the knob. Barely breathing, he studied the dimly lit cellar at the bottom of the stairs but saw no sign of the woman he was following. Confused, he spun around, saw nothing in the dark church, and cursed himself for being so careful. No one, woman or man, was going to stop him from finding his Rita.

Vito heard her labored moans before he reached the bottom of the stairs. In the weak light, he saw her. Rats scrambled for cover as he squeezed into the space between an ancient boiler and the cot where his daughter lay half-covered by a filthy blanket. Her eyes were closed. The left side of her face was purple and swollen. "Rita, speak to me," Vito pleaded. Reaching for her hand, he found her fingers resting on the long handle of a rusted pipe wrench. He slipped it away from her, curious and confused. It was solid and heavy and felt completely at home in the hand of a man who had spent his life working with tools. Rita stirred and moved her lips but did not open her eyes. Vito wanted to pick her up and hold her in his arms but was afraid she might be too badly injured. He needed an ambulance. With his complete attention focused on getting help for his daughter, he had completely forgotten about the woman who had led him to this hell hole.

Olga watched Vito from under the stairs where she had hidden the second the creaking of the old floor upstairs signaled his presence. She had no idea who he was, but she saw him reach for his phone and knew what a call for help would mean for her and her chances of pocketing the small fortune that had become an obsession. Her elbow still hurt from when that little bitch on the cot hit her with something as hard as steel, but there was no time to worry about that now. She charged out of the dark like a bull.

Vito had the cell phone in one hand and the pipe wrench in the other when Olga slammed him into the boiler, shaking clouds of dust from the maze of rusty pipes bolted to it. The phone fell to the floor, but he managed to hang onto the wrench.

Olga had fought male wrestlers in a dozen locker room brawls, and she knew from experience where they were the most vulnerable. Vito sensed the knee coming and twisted in time to take the bruising blow on the side of his thigh. Olga swung wildly with her good arm, sensing that this man had a lot more fight in him than the oiled show-boaters she had encountered on the wrestling circuit. Vito raised his arm to block her rock-like blows, and when he did, he became aware of the deadly weight of the old wrench. Woman or man, he didn't have time to fight. Rita needed an ambulance.

The first blow knocked Olga senseless. The second one splintered her skull. As he watched the woman slump to the trash-strewn floor, Vito saw that she was wearing Rita's baseball jacket. As much as he wanted to yank it from her body and beat her with the wrench until his arms ached, he had a daughter who needed him. He grabbed Olga by the ankles and dragged her out of the way, searching for his cell phone. By the time he found it, Vito had changed his mind about calling 911. He pressed Anthony's speed-dial number.

"Where are you?"

"On my way home. Just passing the Old Line Diner," Anthony answered.

"Perfect. There's a phone booth in the parking lot out front. Pull over and use it to call an ambulance." Vito touched Rita's hair and began to choke up. "Tell them there is a seriously injured woman in the cellar of the old church on Woodyard Road," he managed, adding, "Use the pay phone, not your cell phone."

"What's going on, Papa? Are you okay?"

"I found your sister. She is going to be fine, but she needs an ambulance right this minute."

Anthony exploded with excitement, but Vito cut him off. He started to say he would tell the family all about it later but realized that he could never tell anyone what he had done. "Please, make the call right now," he pleaded. "And, Anthony, never say a word about this conversation to anyone. Ever."

Vito knew he didn't have much time. He knelt beside his unconscious daughter, kissed her, rushed a prayer, and quickly looked around. His mind raced, making a checklist. He knew that when the ambulance crew told the police about this place, T.J. Barnes and his people would turn it upside-down. Thanks to his habit of wearing work gloves, there wouldn't be any fingerprints. What else? he asked himself as the seconds slipped away. The wrench he had hit the woman with. Take that. He stood over Olga's body, wondering if there was anything about it that could lead the police to him. Traces on her knuckles? Skin under her fingernails? He couldn't take a chance. He begged God to hold Rita in His arms until the ambulance arrived and started up the stairs, lugging a dead body as heavy as a bag of rocks. A plan for getting rid of it seemed to come out of nowhere. He would have to think it through, but right now, he was completely focused on making sure that his daughter got to the hospital.

Down at the railroad crossing, an ambulance with pulsing lights separated itself from a myriad of other emergency vehicles and started up the hill toward the church. Vito saw it, said a prayer of thanksgiving, and dumped Olga's body into the back of his truck. Without turning on his lights he drove back to the road, thanked God again when he saw that the florist shop was closed for the night, and pulled into its empty parking lot.

The minutes the ambulance crew spent inside the church were like hours to Vito. There was nothing he could do but pray as hard as he ever prayed in his life. He prayed to The Blessed Mother and to an alphabet of saints from Aloysius to Vitus, the patron saint of every Vito in the world he had been informed in grade school. "Protect my beautiful Rita," he begged them all. "Protect her and make her well. Bring her home to her family, and I will…" There had always been a second part to prayers like these, a donation, a promise, a resolve to become a better person, but

Vito did not know if promises like that counted when they were made by a man who had just killed another human being. Sooner or later, he would own up to what he had done in confession and dumbfound some poor priest, but right now, saying he was sorry would be a lie. As far as he was concerned, anyone who did what that woman had done to his little girl deserved to die. Vito made the sign of the cross and hoped for the best, knowing the repair of his soul would be a project he might not live long enough to pull off.

In the nighttime distance, the figures returning to the ambulance were too small to have faces or even heights and weights. Vito wondered if Dario was one of them. If he was, Vito knew he would ride in the back with his sister, hold her hand, and talk to her all the way to the hospital. The ambulance passed within fifty yards of where he hid in the dark, its emergency lights turning his truck red for two beats of his pounding heart. With the siren fading in the distance, Vito slipped out of the truck and tossed the wrench into the bed next to the woman's body. As he covered them with a concrete curing tarp, he saw the shovel he had found earlier at the plaza site. He lifted it, felt its workman-like weight, and knew exactly what he was going to do.

43

"Let's have coffee on the porch before you leave; it's absolutely beautiful outside," Mary Beth suggested, straightening the lapel pins on T.J.'s uniform.

"Maybe a cup," he said, holding the door open for her.

"Are you sure you can't take the morning off?"

T.J. shook his head. "Too much going on. A contractor is due at the station to remove those plywood window panels that have been there since the hurricane." He smiled. "I better be there to protect him from what Helen might do if he doesn't treat them like priceless works of art."

Mary Beth laughed. "And Skinny Babcock, what's up with him?"

T.J. finished his coffee and pretended to look under the picnic table for eavesdroppers. "Nobody is supposed to know about that," he whispered.

What nobody was supposed to know was that Helen Burgess, a huge Jimmy Buffett fan, had run into the county executive in the parking lot of a concert at

Nationals Park in Washington. The big news was not that Skinny was wearing a parrot hat and Margaritaville tee shirt but that he was holding hands with Councilperson June Buggs-Vosbeck. The negotiations that took place after June fled the scene stipulated that if Helen kept quiet about what she had seen—a promise she had more or less kept—Skinny would arrange for the county to pay for new police station windows and give the painted plywood panels to Helen.

"You would look cute in a parrot hat," Mary Beth kidded T.J. as she took his empty cup.

"Maybe I can borrow Skinny's," he smiled, giving her a peck on the cheek that had become as natural for him as breathing. "Got to run," he said, checking his watch. "I have to stop at the carnival grounds on my way in. The company that is hauling the last of the rides up to Allentown is supposed to be there this morning."

"What's going to happen to them?"

"They'll be auctioned off along with the tents and everything else. A judge up in Pennsylvania has ruled that Olga Muntz is legally dead."

"And you? What do you think?" Mary Beth asked, following him into the kitchen where he took his gun belt and hat from the closet.

T.J. shrugged, reluctant to go down that road again. "I'll be home in plenty of time to pick you up for the plaza dedication."

"We should leave here by two-thirty. Rita Anselmo wants us to sit near her and her family."

The Carnival

The Ferris wheel had been dismantled and was being loaded onto a long flatbed trailer when T.J. pulled onto the carnival grounds. Everything else, tents, generators, popcorn machines, and the beat-up school busses that served as dormitories for Olga Muntz's motley crew, was gone. In the middle of the matted grass field, a pile of junk, chest-high and a good ten yards across, waited for the county sanitation crew to arrive and haul it to the dump.

T.J. got out of his cruiser and leaned against the fender. Except for one major loose end, the nightmare was over. The birds and squirrels, stirring impatiently in the trees, would make short work of the scattered popcorn and peanuts, the grass would bounce back before winter came, and the Muntz Traveling Carnival would become a very bad memory. He hoped that the fire department and everyone else had finally had their fill of carnivals, but if they ever tried to hold another one, he would remind them about a beautiful young nurse named Patricia Dugan and the terrible experience the Anselmo family had lived through because of this one. If that didn't work… If that didn't work… He thought about that for a minute. If that didn't work, he would know it was time to turn in his badge and open the sporting goods store that sat at the end of his rainbow.

"Okay for us to take this now, T.J.?" The question, hollered across the empty field, interrupted pleasant thoughts of outfitting soccer teams and selling kids their first baseball gloves.

Jerry Donnelly and one of his men were inspecting the large wire barrel filled with raffle tickets. "If you and your people are done with this thing, we'll haul it to the firehouse and schedule another drawing." he yelled. "Never did get a chance to pull the winning ticket on the Harley."

"Take it, Jerry. We're finished with it."

"Thanks, T.J. Any sign of Ape Woman?"

Reality returned. T.J. shook his head. Olga Muntz, the Ape Woman, the Allentown Amazon, or whatever else the TV and newspaper people chose to call her, had disappeared. Her beat-up Ford Bronco was locked up in the county impound yard. Her purple *Muntz Travelling Carnival* jacket was hanging in an evidence locker at the police station. Both had been found the night an ambulance crew responded to an anonymous call and rescued Rita Anselmo from the cellar of the old Woodyard Road church. His eyes found the spot where Olga's trailer had been parked, a pigsty on wheels that he had personally turned upside down before letting the trucking company haul it away. Only a hundred yards of trees and underbrush separated the trailer and the windowless cellar where Rita Anselmo had been imprisoned and where, it had become sadly clear, Patricia Dugan had spent her final hours on earth. T.J. had retraced those hundred yards a dozen times, sometimes on his knees. All he had found were traces of footprints that, like the tire tracks in the church parking lot, had been softened beyond usefulness by the same rainstorm that wiped out Jerry Donnelly's raffle.

T.J. slid back into his cruiser. He knew who had found Rita in that cellar. He couldn't prove it, but there was absolutely no doubt in his mind. It was the same guy who could tell him what had happened to Olga Muntz. The police officer in him wanted to talk to Vito Anselmo again, but he had already questioned him three times, sensitively, he hoped, but aggressively enough to test the patience of a man who considered the whole ugly mess history now that his family was whole again.

Much to the displeasure of the feasting birds and squirrels, the crew from the sanitation department arrived and got busy transferring what was left of the carnival into two very large dump trucks. Anybody with the brains of one of those squirrels, T.J. lectured himself, would be satisfied to do what everyone else seemed very happy to do and move on. Maybe it was the thing to do, he told himself again. In the meantime, he had to get to the station before Helen and the window contractor got into it, try to put a dent in the pile of work on his desk, then get home in time to take Mary Beth to the dedication ceremony at the hospital.

44

"Did you ever hear anything more about the man who was killed at the railroad crossing last summer?" Mary Beth asked as they drove to the dedication.

T.J. shook his head. "Nothing since the Illinois State Police wrapped up their investigation."

Through his fingerprints and license plates, the man killed on the railroad tracks had been identified easily enough, but the reason for his being so far away from home while driving a van customized to look like an ambulance remained a strange mystery. Weeks of searching the underbrush along the tracks had resulted in the recovery of almost sixty-seven thousand dollars, money that was apparently in the van when the train obliterated it. T.J. had already told Mary Beth all of this, but he repeated the information patiently, weighing each fact once again as he did. He was silent for a minute before adding, "If he had a cell phone, it was lost in the train wreck."

"Lester Turner. Wasn't that his name?"

"Lester Simpson Turner," T.J. nodded. "White male, seventy-three years old. Rich as hell. Owned a huge house on Lake Michigan north of Chicago. No relatives."

"How about the wrestling thing?"

T.J. shrugged as they slowed for a light. "Nothing new on that. Turner managed professional wrestlers when he was younger, apparently as a hobby more than anything else. Olga Muntz was one of his stars, but that was many years ago, and no one has found any evidence to connect the two of them since she left the ring."

"Could be a coincidence."

"Could be but add the wrestling thing to Lester Turner showing up the same day the ambulance crew found Rita Anselmo in that old church, and it all begins to sound like a detective story with a missing chapter."

"How dramatic of you."

"Did I mention the missing body?" T.J. meant the question to sound like a joke but didn't do a very good job of it.

Traffic slowed as they got close to the hospital and was bumper to bumper by the time they reached the parking lot entrance where Mark Jenkins was directing traffic. "Afternoon, Chief," he said, leaning toward the car window and smiling at Mary Beth. "We saved a parking space for you right next to the plaza."

"The perks of power," T.J. smiled as the young sergeant waived them through.

The hospital's new plaza was arguably the nicest space in Hargrove County, praise that one newspaper columnist dampened by pointing out that its closest competition was the food court at Hargrove Mall. A light fall breeze wandered through a ring of freshly planted maples, launching a confetti of red leaves into the surprisingly large crowd gathering for the dedication. It might not have been Rockefeller Center, but the new plaza was no food court. Geometrically scored concrete paving inside the circle of trees was arranged with carved granite benches, boulevard-style light fixtures, and an imported fountain even larger than the one in Vito Anselmo's front yard. Because of the natural spring that had been uncovered during construction, the concrete under the fountain itself was more massive than a mountain boulder. These details, minus the reference to Vito's house, were listed in the official dedication program, as were the names and slightly overstated profiles of the hospital board members and every county council member except for June Buggs-Vosbeck who, it was believed, had moved to Idaho.

Because there were so many of them, the Anselmo family arrived at the hospital in two vehicles, a big Mercedes that spent most of its life in the Anselmo garage and Anthony's work truck. Vincenzo, the grandfather, had been invited to ride in the truck with his grandsons but insisted on squeezing into the back seat of the Mercedes so he could sit next to the granddaughter he did not want out of his sight.

"I'm good, Nanu," Rita assured him often. "The bad woman is gone."

"She come back. Like a devil, she come back," he insisted, despite constant assurances from his son, Vito, that she never would.

As they walked together from the parking lot, Vincenzo held Rita's hand like she was a little girl and eyed Mary Beth warily when she approached to greet his granddaughter with a hug. A very gentle hug. Her bruises and swollen face were by now just an unsettling memory, but Mary Beth knew that Rita's neck and shoulders still bothered her more than she would admit.

"The balloons were a wonderful idea," Mary Beth said.

With the blessing of Martha Richardson, the best-selling author who had donated the money for the plaza, plans for its dedication had been modified to include a tribute to Patricia Dugan who had lost her life so senselessly during what a local television reporter had labeled The Carnival from Hell. Twenty-four blue balloons, one for each year of Patricia's short life, were to be released while the author herself led a prayer for the repose of the young nurse's soul.

"Isn't that your uncle Phil handing out the balloons?"

Rita nodded. "He paid for them and for the printing of the programs with that beautiful picture of Patricia on the back cover."

"That was very generous of him," Mary Beth answered. She was tempted to say something about the Palermo Cadillac advertisement at the bottom of the same page but managed to hold her tongue. "Very generous," she repeated.

What nobody but Phil Palermo knew was that he had promised a little more than he could deliver for the safe return of his niece Rita and was currently in negotiations with God who he hoped would settle for the cost of the balloons, the printing of the program, and a twenty-five dollar increase in his Sunday donations from now until the First Sunday of Advent.

While Vito Anselmo waited for his daughter and father to catch up with the rest of the family, he stood at a spot about halfway between the fountain and the VIP chairs, staring silently at something near his feet.

"Lose something?" T.J. asked, extending his hand.

Vito shook T.J.'s hand but didn't say anything, a reaction T.J. understood and hoped would change as time passed. T.J. had done what he felt he had to do during a very difficult period for the Anselmo family. With Vito's permission, and on the finger-in-the-chest condition that he "take it easy with her," T.J. had questioned Rita as soon as the doctors in the emergency room gave him the green light. Twice, he had asked Vito about the night Rita had been found in the church cellar.

"What do you want from me, Barnes?" Vito had exploded the second time. "My beautiful daughter was taken away from her family. Now she is back. What more is there to know?"

"The woman who hurt your daughter, the woman who we are sure killed the Dugan girl, we need to find her."

"Find her then."

T.J. was lost in thought as a tall woman, dressed in what he would have described as hippie clothes, removed her very large eyeglasses and spoke about her mother, the plaza, and the generous donation Vito Anselmo had made to establish the Patricia Ann Dugan Nursing Scholarship. He did not notice Vito's wife, Marie, whispering for him to stand up when he was recognized. What he did notice was Vito's trance-like concentration on an area of the concrete paving a few feet in front of where he and his family were sitting. T.J. wished he were a mind reader or had the intelligence of a Sherlock Holmes or a Walt Longmire, whose cases were the only programs besides ball games he ever watched on television.

A light fall breeze pushed a fallen leaf across the plaza. It rested for a second on the spot marked by Vito's laser-like stare before moving on. Vito's eyes did not follow it. His heart, his soul, and every fiber of his being overflowed with anger so intense that it was painful. He wanted to do again what he had done to the animal who had been ready to kill his beautiful Rita as savagely and senselessly as she had killed that poor girl Patricia.

A prayer was said, the blue balloons were released, and as the people around him began to leave, Vito's eyes narrowed to slits. *Goddamn you to hell,* he cursed deep within himself, staring down into Olga's unseeing eyes. The thick mass of concrete that entombed her did not keep him from seeing her lying on her back in Rita's bloodied baseball jacket. He saw the heavy wrench next to her head where it landed when he hurled it into the dark hole before working feverishly through the night, shoveling gravel to hide the evidence of his vengeance from the work crew that would seal the excavation with tons of wet concrete. He knew what T.J. Barnes would never know. He knew where Olga would spend eternity. Standing up, he cursed quietly in Italian and spit on the concrete plaza at his feet.

"Vito, what are you doing?" Marie asked in a shocked whisper.

He took her hand. "Let's go home," he said.

As T.J. watched the Anselmos cross the driveway and disappear into the parking lot, he had the strange feeling that he was watching the end of a story whose message was "All's well that ends well." It was a thought that had come out of nowhere and would not go away.

"Let it go," Mary Beth told him leaning her head against his shoulder. "Like they say, all's well that ends well."

T.J. twisted the wedding band that still felt strange on his finger, realizing that living with a woman who could read his mind was going to be very tricky business.

www.ingramcontent.com/pod-product-compliance
Lightning Source LLC
LaVergne TN
LVHW091632070526
838199LV00044B/1036